Joseph O'Connor was born in Dublin. He has written thirteen books, including six novels: *Cowboys and Indians*, *Desperadoes*, *The Salesman*, *Inishowen*, *Star of the Sea*, which became an international bestseller, winning the *Irish Post* Award for Literature, an American Library Association Award, France's Prix Millepages and the Prix Madeleine Zepter for European Novel of the Year and, most recently, *Redemption Falls*. His work has been published in twenty-nine languages.

ALSO BY JOSEPH O'CONNOR

Novels

Cowboys and Indians

Desperadoes

The Salesman

Inishowen

Star of the Sea

Redemption Falls

Short Stories/Novellas

The Comedian

Non-fiction

Even the Olives are Bleeding: The Life and Times of Charles Donnelly

The Secret World of the Irish Male

The Irish Male at Home and Abroad

Sweet Liberty: Travels in Irish America

The Last of the Irish Males

Stage Plays

Red Roses and Petrol

The Weeping of Angels

True Believers (adaptation)

Screenplays

A Stone of the Heart

The Long Way Home

Ailsa

Editor

Yeats is Dead! A Serial Novel by Fifteen Irish Writers

JOSEPH O'CONNOR

True Believers

VINTAGE BOOKS
London

Published by Vintage 2008

2 4 6 8 10 9 7 5 3 1

First published in Great Britain in 1991 by
Sinclair-Stevenson Ltd

Vintage
Random House, 20 Vauxhall Bridge Road,
London SW1V 2SA

www.vintage-books.co.uk

Addresses for companies within The Random House Group Limited
can be found at: www.randomhouse.co.uk/offices.htm

The Random House Group Limited Reg. No. 954009

A CIP catalogue record for this book
is available from the British Library

ISBN 9780099498315

The Random House Group Limited supports The Forest Stewardship
Council (FSC®), the leading international forest certification organisation.
Our books carrying the FSC label are printed on FSC® certified paper.
FSC is the only forest certification scheme endorsed by the leading
environmental organisations, including Greenpeace. Our
paper procurement policy can be found at
www.randomhouse.co.uk/environment

Printed and bound in Great Britain by Clays Ltd, St Ives PLC

TO
SEAN AND VIOLA

ACKNOWLEDGEMENTS

My first two published stories, 'Last of the Mohicans' and 'Ailsa', appeared in *The Sunday Tribune*, Dublin, in January and November 1989. I owe a great debt of gratitude to the editor of the New Irish Writing page, Ciaran Carty.

'Last of the Mohicans' also appeared in Ryan Publishing's *Forgiveness: Voices One*. Thanks to David Ryan and Professor Gus Martin.

Characters and ideas from these and some other early stories – especially 'Mothers Were All the Same' – reappear in my first novel, *Cowboys and Indians*.

'Freedom of the Press' was first published in *The Irish Times*, July 1990. Many thanks to Caroline Walshe.

'The Wizard of Oz' was first published in *Iron* magazine, Tyne and Wear, England. Many thanks to the editor, Peter Mortimer.

Many thanks to Bernard and Mary Loughlin at the Tyrone Guthrie Centre, Annaghmakerrig, County Monaghan, Ireland, under whose hallowed roof several of these stories were conceived.

Very many thanks to everyone at Sinclair-Stevenson, still the grooviest publishers in town. Also to my agent Lisa Eveleigh, Michael O'Riordan, Paddy Breathnach, and, as always, Marie O'Riordan. And my greatest thanks to my father Sean and my stepmother Viola, for their constant help and encouragement.

CONTENTS

I would thou wert cold or hot. So then because thou art lukewarm, and neither cold nor hot, I will spue thee out of my mouth.

REVELATION 3:16

Last of the Mohicans

IT WAS about three years since I'd seen him. And here he was, sweating behind the burger bar in Euston Station, a vision in polyester and fluorescent light. Jesus Christ, so Marion was right that time. Eddie Virago, selling double cheeseburgers for a living. I spluttered his name as he smiled in puzzled recognition over the counter. My God, Eddie Virago. In the pub he kept saying it was great to see me. Really wild, he said. I should have let him know I was coming to London. This was just unreal.

Eddie was the kind of guy I tried to hang around with in college. Suave, cynical, dressed like a Sunday supplement. He'd arrive deliberately late for lectures and swan into Theatre L, permanent pout on his lips. He sat beside me one day in the first week and asked me for a light. Then he asked me for a cigarette. From then on we were friends. After pre-revolutionary France we'd sit on the middle floor of the canteen sipping coffee and avoiding Alice, the tea-trolley lady.

'Where did you get that tray?' she'd whine. 'No trays upstairs.' And Eddie would interrupt his monologue on the role of German Expressionism in the development of *film noir* to remove his feet from the perilous path of her brush. 'Alice's Restaurant', he called it. I didn't know what he was talking about, but I laughed anyway.

He was pretty smart, our Eddie. He was a good-looking bastard, too. I never realised it at first, but gradually I noticed all the girls in the class wanted to get to know me. Should have known it wasn't me they were interested in.

'Who's your friend?' they'd simper, giggling like crazy.

The rugby girls really liked him. You know the type. The ones who sit in the corridors calculating the cost of the lecturers' suits. All school scarves, dinner dances, summers in New York without a visa – so much more exciting that way. Eddie hated them all. He resisted every coy advance, every uncomfortable, botched flirtation. They were bloody convent schoolgirls. All talk and no action. He said there was just one thing they needed and they weren't going to get it from him.

Professor Gough liked making risqué jokes about the nocturnal activities of Napoleon and everyone in the class was shocked. Everyone except Eddie. He'd laugh out loud and drag on his cigarette and laugh again while everyone blushed and stared at him. He said that was the trouble with Ireland. He said we were all hung up about sex. It was unhealthy. It was no wonder the mental homes were brimming over.

Eddie had lost his virginity at the age of fourteen, in a thatched cottage in Kerry. Next morning, he'd shaved with a real razor and he'd felt like a real man. As the sun dawned on his manhood he had flung his scabby old electric into the Atlantic. Then himself and his nineteen-year-old deflowerer ('deflorist', he called her) had strolled down the beach talking about poetry. She'd written to him from France a few times, but he'd never answered. It didn't do to get too involved. All of Western civilisation was hung up on possession, Eddie said. People had to live their own lives and get away from guilt trips.

We were close, Eddie and me. I bought him drinks and cigarettes, and he let me stay in his place when I got kicked out that time. His parents gave him the money to live in a flat in Donnybrook. He called them his 'old dears'. I went back home after a while but I never forgot my two weeks on the southside with Eddie. We stayed up late looking at films and listening to The Doors and The Jesus and Mary Chain and talking about sex. Eddie liked to talk about sex a lot. He said I didn't know what was ahead of me. He was amazed that I hadn't done it. Absolutely amazed. He envied me actually, because if he had it all to do over again the first time was definitely the best. But that was Catholic Ireland. We were all repressed, and we had to escape. James Joyce was right. Snot green sea, what a line. It wasn't the same in India, he said. Sex was divine to them. They had their priorities right.

Eddie went away that summer, to Germany, and he came back with a gaggle of new friends. They were all in Trinity, and they'd worked in the same gherkin factory as him. They were big into drugs and funny haircuts and Ford Fiestas. Eddie had the back and sides of his head shaved and he let his fringe grow down over his eyes and he dyed it. Alice the tea trolley lady would cackle at him in the canteen.

'Would you look!' she'd scoff. 'The last of the Mohicans.'

Everyone laughed but Eddie didn't care. He didn't even blush. He rubbed glue and toothpaste into his quiff to make it stand up, and even in the middle of the most crowded room you could always tell where Eddie was. His orange hair bobbed on a sea of short back and sides.

He went to parties in his new friends' houses, and they all slept with each other. No strings attached. No questions asked. He brought me to one of them once, in a big house in Dalkey. Lots of glass everywhere, that's all I remember. Lots of glass. And paintings on the walls, by Louis Le Brocquy and that other guy who's always painting his penis. You know the one. That was where I met Marion. She was in the kitchen, searching the fridge while two philosophy students groped each other under the table. She didn't like these parties much. We sat in the garden eating cheese sandwiches and drinking beer. Eddie stumbled out and asked me if I wanted a joint. I said no, I wasn't in the mood. Marion got up to leave with some bloke in a purple shirt who was muttering about deconstruction. Eddie said he wouldn't know the meaning of the word.

We bumped into her again at a gig in The Underground one Sunday night. It turned out the deconstructionist was her brother and he was in the band. When she asked me what I thought, I said they were pretty interesting. She thought they were terrible. I bought her a drink and she asked me back to her place in Rathmines. In the jacks I whispered to Eddie that I didn't want him tagging along. He said he got the picture. Standing on the corner of Stephen's Green he winked at us and said, 'Goodnight young lovers, and if you can't be good, be careful.'

It wasn't at all like Eddie said it would be. Afterwards I laughed when she asked me had it been my first time. Was she kidding? I'd lost it in a cottage in Kerry when I was fourteen. She smiled and said yes, she'd only been kidding. All night long I tossed and turned in her single bed, listening to the police cars outside. I couldn't wait to tell Eddie about it.

We went for breakfast in Bewleys the next morning. Me and Marion, I mean. She looked different without make-up. I felt embarrassed as she walked around the flat in tights and underwear. It was months later that I admitted I'd been lying about my sexual experience. She laughed and said she'd known all along. She said I paid far too much attention to Eddie. That was our first row. She said that for someone who wasn't hung up, he sure talked a lot of bullshit about it.

At first Eddie was alright about Marion and me. I told him we had done it and he clapped me on the back and asked me how it was. I said I knew what he'd been talking about. It'd been unreal. That was the only word for it. He nodded wisely and asked me something about positions. I said I had to go to a lecture.

But as I started spending more and more time with Marion he got more sarcastic. He started asking me how was the little woman, and what was it like to be happily married. He got a big kick out of it and it made me squirm. He'd introduce me to another one of the endless friends.

'This is Johnny,' he'd say, 'he's strictly monogamous.'

We still went for coffee after lectures, but I felt more and more alone in the company of Eddie and his disciples. Marion took me to anti-amendment meetings and Eddie said we were wasting our time. He said it didn't make any difference. Irish people took their direction straight from the Catholic Church. He told me we hadn't a hope.

'Abortion?' he said. 'Jesus Christ, we're not even ready for contraception.'

I tried to tell him it wasn't just about abortion, but he scoffed and said he'd heard it all before.

Eddie dropped out a few months before our finals. He left a note on my locker door saying he'd had enough. He was going to London to get into film. Writing mainly, but he hoped to direct, of course, in the end. London was where the action was. He was sick and tired of this place anyway. It was nothing. A glorified tax haven for rich tourists and popstars. A cultural backwater that time forgot. He said no one who ever did anything stayed in Ireland. You had to get out to be recognised.

I was sad to see him go, specially because he couldn't even tell me to my face. But in a way it was a relief. Me and Eddie, we'd grown far apart. It wasn't that I didn't like him exactly. I just knew that secretly we embarrassed the hell out of each other. So I screwed his note into a ball and went off to the library. And as I sat staring out the window at the lake and the concrete, I tried my best to forget all about him.

Marion broke it off with me the week before the exams started. She said no hard feelings but she reckoned we'd run our course. I congratulated her on her timing. We were walking through Stephen's Green and the children were bursting balloons and hiding behind the statues. She said she just didn't know where we were going any more. I said I didn't know about her, but I was going to Madigan's. She said that was the kind of thing Eddie would have said, and I felt really good about that. She kissed me on the cheek, said sorry and sloped off down Grafton Street. I felt the way you do when the phone's just been slammed down on you. I thought if one of those Hare Krishnas comes near me I'll kick his bloody head in.

I got a letter from Eddie once. Just once. He said he was getting on fine, but it was taking a while to meet the right people. Still, he was glad he'd escaped 'the stifling provincialism' and he regretted nothing. He was having a wild time and there was so much to do in London. Party City. And the women! Talk about easy. I never got around to answering him. Well, I was still pretty upset about Marion for a while, and then there was all that hassle at home. I told them I'd be only too happy to get out and look for a job if there were any jobs to look for. My father said that was fine talk, and that the trouble with me was that they'd been too bloody soft on me. He'd obviously wasted his time, subsidising my idleness up in that bloody place that was supposedly a university.

Eventually it all got too much. I moved in with Alias, into an upstairs flat on Leeson Street. My mother used to cry when I went home to do my washing on Sunday afternoons. Alias was a painter. I met him at one of Eddie's parties. The walls of the flat were plastered with paintings of naked bodies, muscles rippling, nipples like champagne corks. He said it didn't matter that they didn't look like the models. Hadn't I ever heard of imagination? I said yeah, I'd heard of it.

He was putting his portfolio together for an exhibition and living on the dole. He told everyone he had an Arts Council grant. He was alright, but he didn't have the depth of Eddie and he was a bit of a slob. He piled up his dirty clothes in the middle of his bedroom floor and he kept his empty wine bottles in the wardrobe. And the bathroom. And the kitchen. I got a job eventually, selling rubbish bags over the phone. There are thirty-seven different sizes of domestic and industrial plastic refuse sack. I bet you didn't know that! I had to ring up factories and offices and ask them if they wanted to re-order. They never seemed to want to. I wondered what they did with all their rubbish.

'Shredders,' said Mr Smart. 'The shredders will be my undoing.'

'Yeah,' I told him, 'you and Oliver North.' He didn't get the joke.

It was always hard to get the right person on the line. Mr Smart said not to fool around with secretaries, go straight for the decision-makers. They always seemed to be tied up though. The pay was nearly all commission too, so I never had much cash to spare. The day I handed in my notice Mr Smart said he was disappointed in me. He thought I would have had a bit more tenacity. I told him to shag off. I said sixty-five pence basic per hour didn't buy much in the way of tenacity.

'Or courtesy either,' he said, tearing up my reference.

That afternoon I ran into Marion on O'Connell Bridge. We went for coffee and had a bit of a laugh. I told her about chucking the job and she said I was dead right. She told me a secret. It wasn't confirmed yet, but fingers crossed. She was going off to Ethiopia. She was sick of just talking. She wanted to do something about the world. If Bob Geldof could do it, why couldn't she? I said it all sounded great, and maybe I'd do the same. Then she asked me all about Alias and the new flat and we talked about the old days. It seemed so long ago. I had almost forgotten what she looked like. She said her friend Mo had just written a postcard from London. She'd seen some guy who looked just like Eddie Virago working in a burger joint in Euston Station. Except he had a short back and sides now. I laughed out loud. Eddie selling hamburgers for a living? Someone of his talent? That would be the day. She said it was nice to get postcards, all the same. She showed it to me. It had a guy on it with a huge red mohican haircut. Mo said she'd bought that one because it reminded her of how Eddie used to look in the old days. She said she'd always fancied him. Marion said she'd send me a card from Ethiopia, if they had them. She never did.

•

In the pub Eddie and I didn't have much to say, except that it was great to see each other. When I told him the postcard story he said it all went to prove you couldn't trust anyone, and he sipped meaningfully at his pint. After closing time we got the Tube up to the West End, to a disco Eddie knew in Soho. Drunks lolled around the platforms, singing and crying. The club was a tiny place with sweat running down the walls. Eddie asked the black bouncer if Eugene was in tonight.

'Who?' said the bouncer.

'You know, Eugene,' Eddie said, 'the manager.'

The bouncer shrugged and said, 'Not tonight, man. I dunno no Eugene.'

I paid Eddie in, because it wasn't his pay day till Thursday. He was really sorry about that.

Downstairs he had to lean across the table, shaking the drinks, to shout in my ear. The writing was going alright. Of course, it was all contacts, all a closed shop, but he was still trying. In fact, he'd just finished a script and although he wasn't free to reveal the details he didn't mind telling me there was quite a bit of interest in it. He only hoped it wasn't too adventurous. Thatcher had the BBC by the short and curlies, he said. They wouldn't take any risks at all. And Channel Four wasn't the same since Isaacs left. Bloody shame that, man of his creative flair.

He'd made lots of friends though, in the business. I'd probably meet them later. They only went out clubbing late at night. Nocturnal animals, he said. It was more cool to do that. They were great people, though. Really wild. Honestly, from Neil Jordan downwards the business was wonderful. Oh sure, he'd met Jordan. He'd crashed at

Eddie's place one night after a particularly wild party. Really decent bloke. There was a good scene in London, too. No, he didn't listen to any of the old bands any more. He was all into Acid House. He said that was this year's thing. Forget The Clash. Guitar groups were out. The word was Acid. I said I hadn't heard any and what was it like? He said you couldn't describe it really. It wasn't the kind of music you could put into words.

I did meet one of his friends later on in the night. He saw her standing across the dance floor and beckoned her over. She mustn't have seen him. So he said he'd be back in a second and he weaved through the gyrating bodies to where she was. They chatted for a few minutes, and then she came over and sat down. Shirley was a model. From Dublin too. Well, trying to make it as a model. She knew Bono really well. He was a great bloke, she said, really dead on. She'd known him and Ali for absolute yonks, and success hadn't changed them at all. 'Course, she hadn't seen them since Wembley last year. Backstage. They were working on the new album apparently. She'd heard the rough mixes and it was a total scorcher. This friend of hers played them to her. A really good friend of hers, actually, who went out with your man from The Hot House Flowers. The one with the hair. She kept forgetting his name. She said she was no good at all for Irish names. She really regretted it, actually, specially since she moved over here, but she couldn't speak a word of Irish. She let us buy her a drink each. I paid for Eddie's. Then she had to run. Early start tomorrow, had to be in the studio by eight-thirty.

'Ciao,' she said, when she went. 'Ciao, Eddie.'

It was after four when they kicked us out. The streets of Soho were jostling with minicabs and hot-dog sellers. A crowd filtered out of Ronnie Scott's, just around the corner. Sleek black women in furs and lace. Tall men in sharp suits. Eddie apologised for his friends not showing up. He said if he'd known I was coming he would have arranged a really wild session. Next time. He knew this really happening hip-hop club up in Camden Town, totally wild, but in a very cool kind of way.

In the coffee bar in Leicester Square he was quiet. The old career hadn't been going exactly to plan. He was getting there alright. But much slower than he thought. Still, that was the business. Things got a bit lonely, he said. He got so frustrated, so down. It was hard being an exile. He didn't want to be pretentious or anything, but he knew how Sam Beckett must have felt. If he didn't believe in himself as much as he did, he didn't know how he could go on. He would have invited me back to his place, only a few people were crashing there, so there just wasn't the room. But next time. Honest. It was a big place, but still, it was always full. People were always just dropping in, unannounced.

'You know how it is,' he laughed.

I ordered two more cappuccinos.

'I have measured out my life in coffee spoons,' he said, and he sipped painfully. He always drank Nicaraguan, actually, at home. Very into the cause. I said I knew nothing about it. He started to tell me all the facts but I said I really had to go. My aunt would be worried sick about me. If I didn't get home soon she'd call the police or something. He nodded and said fair enough. He had to split as well.

We stood in the rain on Charing Cross Road while he scribbled his address on a soggy beermat. He told me it was good to see me again. I told him I nearly didn't recognise him with the new haircut. Oh that, he'd had to get rid of that, for work. Anyway, punk was dead. It was all history now.

'You should come over here for good,' he said, 'it's a great city.'

I shook his hand and said I'd think about it. He told me not to let the opportunity pass me by.

The taxi driver asked me where I wanted to go. He loved Ireland. The wife was half Irish and they'd been over a few times now. Lovely country. Terrible what was going on over there, though. He said they were bloody savages. Bloody cowboys and Indians. No offence, but he just couldn't understand it. I said I couldn't either. In his opinion it was all to do with religion.

By the time we got to Greenwich the sun was painting the sky over the river. He said he hoped I enjoyed the rest of my holiday. I hadn't any money left to give him a tip.

Mothers Were All the Same

I MET Catriona again on the train in from Luton. I had noticed her on the plane, just before we came in to land, leafing through the lousy in-flight magazine – 'a great big top o'the morning from Delaney's Irish Cabaret' – while the old lady beside her worried about air disasters. The hostess told her to calm down and held her bony little hand. The old lady's hand, that is. Not Catriona's. Catriona's hands weren't bony at all. They were cute.

She said it was statistically impossible. She said you had more chance of being kicked to death by a mule than dying in an air crash. The old lady said to tell that to Yuri Gagarin, but the hostess just giggled and said, 'Who's he when he's at home? Something to do with glasnost, is it?' Catriona looked over at me. She grinned, and she rolled her beautiful eyes.

The plane screeched in, bucked as the wheels skimmed the ground, and shuddered to a halt outside the arrivals terminal. Catriona was ahead of me as we shuffled in off the tarmac, collars raised in the cold. Two police cars emptied. The plainclothes men stared and scribbled like crazy on their clipboards as we filed past them.

I told the customs guy I'd just arrived from Dublin, and I didn't know how long I'd be staying. That was true alright. He glared under his peaked cap, making me feel guilty. He had a face like the 'Spitting Image' puppet of Norman Tebbit, but without the charm. I mean, I hadn't done anything, but the way he looked at me made me feel like some kind of terrorist, just the same. Then he asked me to write down my full name, and he slouched off into a back room. That's it, I thought, I'm finished now. I gazed around the baggage lounge, full of wailing babies and neon signs. LUTON: GATEWAY TO THE SOUTH EAST. RYANAIR TO THE REPUBLIC OF IRELAND. LOADZA LUVVERLY LOLLY IN THE SIZZLING SOARAWAY SUN. Then I saw her staring at me. Just for a second, but she was definitely looking at me. I smiled back, but she turned away to look for her bags. I made up my mind to ask her later, if I got the chance.

'Right,' said the customs man, and he told me to report my address to the local police as soon as I had one. I was going to ask why. But you don't bother, do you? You're so relieved that your name hasn't somehow crept into their bloody computer that you just smile politely and say thanks very much. He said he hoped I had a nice trip, and he was sorry for holding me up. But it was for everyone's good, if I knew what he meant. I knew what he meant.

I only had my rucksack, so I caught up with her on the other side of customs. I saw her immediately, looking in the window of the Sock Shop.

A troop of boy scouts was lined up at the burger counter, screaming curses and waving banknotes. Three football fans were drunk and singing in the corner, beer all over their England shirts. Soldiers walked up and down with machine guns in their hands. Actually, there were uniforms everywhere, now that I think of it. That's one thing I noticed straightaway, everybody seemed to be wearing a uniform. Customs, police, pilots, cleaners, waitresses, delivery boys, hostesses, all rushing around the hall. Above it all was the sound of the loudspeaker, announcing late flights and missing passengers.

I said, 'Excuse me,' and she turned around, looking a little surprised.

'Yeah?' she said.

I asked if I had seen her somewhere before. I was hoping she wouldn't think this was some big corny pick-up line, but I really did think I had seen her somewhere before and I couldn't remember where. I said I couldn't help noticing her on the plane and she looked familiar. She said she really didn't think so, and she looked away. I said I was sure. She turned again and scrutinised me. Then she asked if I was a friend of Johnny Reilly, by any chance. I said, yeah, I was. Used to be anyway. Recognition dawned on her face. That party he had – last Christmas? I was there with a blond-haired girl. Susan. Yes. She remembered me now. I was pretty flattered, actually, until she pointed out the reason she remembered me. I was the one who had puked over the aspidistra in the hall.

I grinned. She pursed her lips and looked at her watch. I said it was a small world. She said, yeah, it was a small world, but she wouldn't like to have to paint it. There didn't seem to be much else to say. She'd just come over for the weekend. What about me? I was here looking for a job. Who wasn't? I told her I didn't know how long I'd stick it. She just kept staring at that watch so eventually I just said bye, and she wished me luck and dragged her case outside to the bus stop for Luton station.

I waited for the next bus. Well, if she wanted to be like that, fine, I didn't really feel like being friendly anyway. Too many things on my mind. I didn't feel like some big conversation. OK, OK, so I had Aunt Martha's place, but that was only good for a few weeks at most, the old bat. I'd have to get a job soon. Then my own place. I never knew the folks would be so upset about me going, either. When I told them first they were delighted. But the morning I left it was a different story. Tears and scribbled addresses and folded-up tenners in the suit pocket. The whole emigrant bit. You'd have sworn I was going to the moon, the way they went on. The whole thing was like some bloody Christy Moore song come to life in our front room. On the way out to the airport I actually thought my father was going to tell me the facts of life. It was that bad.

At least the suit wasn't too hick. Still fitted me, anyway. Just about. Though I'd really have to go on a diet. All the drinking I'd done in the weeks I was saying my goodbyes was catching up fast. I must have put on eight pounds. But everyone insists on buying you pints, so what can you do? Everyone except Johnny Reilly, of course, the tight shit. My father got me the suit the week I started college. It was hanging over the back of my door when I reeled in that night. He said I'd need a good suit. I wore it twice in three years. Once for Granny's funeral and once for my graduation. He said to bring it with me to London anyway. He said I'd need it for all the interviews.

On the bus I thought about Una Murray. I'd never known she was into me until it was too late. But after our farewell drink she lunged at me on Capel Street Bridge, with the wind from the Liffey blowing through her hair like in a movie or something. Shit. If only I'd known before. Well, it wouldn't have made any difference. Still, would have been nice to know. Susan would have been jealous as hell.

When I got to Luton station, the London train was just pulling in, and the scramble of passengers was milling around the doorways. I fought my way on, dragging the rucksack behind, and I made a rush for the one spare seat. There were posters everywhere, saying that unattended luggage would be removed by the cops and blown up.

There she was, sitting opposite me as I squeezed in. Catriona. She was reading a book. *The Ultimate Good Luck* by Richard Ford. She looked up and smiled again. She said we must stop meeting like this. I tried to think of something smart but nothing came. I just grinned back like an idiot and I think I blushed as I offered her a duty-free cigarette. She shook her head and took off her glasses and pointed to another sign. NO SMOKING. An old man with a moustache glared at me.

'Haven't you heard of King's Cross?' he said.

We got talking again. She asked me where I was staying in London. Strange, but I said I didn't know. I don't know why I said that. Because I did know. But as Johnny Reilly says, I can't give anyone a straight answer, and I must admit that much is true. I suppose I was afraid she'd have nowhere to stay and want to come to Aunt Martha's with me. Look, I know it's stupid, but I'm funny like that. I like my space. Crazy, I know, but what can you do? I think it's because everyone at home asks so many bloody questions. Where were you? Until when? Who were you with? And the great bloody existential conundrum of course: just who do you think you are? All that stuff is enough to make anyone defensive. I'm not saying it's right. I'm just saying that's the way it is.

I needn't have worried. She was fixed up already, staying in some hotel near the station. It was a small place, she said, but it was hunky-dory. I couldn't remember the last time I'd heard that expression. Hunky-dory. As the train pulled in I asked if she needed any help with her bags. I knew she didn't, but I thought I'd ask anyway. She said she could manage on her own. So I shook hands with her on the platform and said goodbye again. Her hand was cold. She smiled, because I was being so formal, I suppose, with the handshake and everything. She said she might see me around. I shrugged and said I hoped so. She told me she hoped I'd find somewhere to stay, and I said good luck, see you, and walked off.

'Eddie,' she shouted, as I walked through the ticket barrier. I turned and saw her trotting towards me, dragging her case, panting. She said she was sorry, that I must have thought she was really rude. I wondered what she meant. She said if I really had nowhere to stay why didn't I come with her? She said that was the obvious thing. She was sure they'd have another room. It was a really cheap place too, and if I needed somewhere to sleep for a few nights, until I found something else, it was probably OK. I hesitated. I knew I couldn't afford to stay in any hotel, no matter how cheap, not even for one night. Three nights would nearly clean me out. But then I thought, to hell with it. Why not?

Nothing ventured, all of that. I just felt like doing something different. I don't know why. Something spontaneous after all the weeks of planning every last moment. That's what I wanted. And I suppose I have to admit I thought she was pretty cute, too. I asked whether she was sure she wouldn't mind. She said, of course not. She'd love the company. I could come with her now, and maybe she could show me some of the sights over the weekend. Alright. I said I would.

She was amazed that I'd never been to London before. She'd come over every summer for three years. She had a job over there whenever she wanted it, in some trendy lefty bookshop on Charing Cross Road. She might come over for good next year, she said. But she knew what it was like to be in London on your own. It was such an overwhelming place. So huge and anonymous and impersonal. So different from Dublin. Yeah, I told her, that's why I came over.

Then she wanted to know what Johnny Reilly was doing these days. I said I didn't know. I was going to tell her about our big falling out, but I didn't bother. I just said I hadn't seen him for a while, and I hadn't a clue what he was up to, but it was probably either illegal or a waste of time.

'That sounds like Johnny alright,' she said.

So we went over together to the El Dorado Hotel and we signed in. The Greek guy behind the counter told us he rented rooms by the hour. You didn't have to have them for the whole night. There were no questions asked here, not blooming likely. I blushed like a sap and she made some joke. The Greek laughed out loud and apologised. Then he said he did have separate rooms to spare and he'd show us the way. Creaking up the stairs I whispered that I wasn't so crazy about this kip. But she told me not to be so silly, that old Zorba was only joking about the hourly rate. I said I thought he was pretty serious, and she sighed and said she knew, but for seven-fifty a night you couldn't expect The Ritz. I coughed knowledgeably and said I supposed she was right.

While she changed and unpacked, I slipped downstairs and outside and phoned Aunt Martha. The phone box was plastered with stickers advertising masseuses and prostitutes and kinky nuns and 'corporal punishment specialists'. I thought it must be great to be a specialist at something. Aunt Martha's businesslike voice buzzed down the line. I was to come over immediately. She had the dinner on and my cousins were just dying to meet me again. I imagined Uncle Frank and her and Alvin and Sharon sitting around the table. I could just see them all – waiting for me. I reconsidered, just for a second.

But I just couldn't face it. I told Aunt Martha I was sorry but I was still in Dublin airport and I couldn't make it until Monday. It was the fog, I said. Everything was screwed up because of the fog. I felt bad about lying, but what can you do? She sounded so disappointed though. Soon as I'd said it, I regretted it, but it was too late then. She said they'd just have to wait. I said I was really sorry. She said she should think so too. All the trouble she'd gone too, not to mention the expense. I noticed her weird accent. She nearly didn't sound Irish at all.

The funny thing was, though, as soon as I put the phone down I knew in my heart that this whole thing was a big mistake. I really did. I just had this feeling, you know? Like God was going to get me for lying to Aunt Martha. Not that I believe in God. But still. You never know.

Back at the El Dorado things were looking up. My room was fine. It was small, but you could see Tower Bridge in the distance, and there was a television in the corner. I flicked the switch but nothing happened. You had to put a pound coin in the slot to make it work. Well, it looked good. And although I didn't want to watch anything, it made me feel good knowing that I could, if I wanted to, if I had a pound to spare.

I sat down and bounced on the bed. Gently. Yeah, this was great. God, I thought, if my mother could only see me now. Holed up with a strange woman in a King's Cross knocking shop. I felt like a Harold Robbins hero.

I said this to Catriona on the Tube up to Leicester Square that night. She said she wasn't familiar with the Harold Robbins *oeuvre* – she was a little sarcastic really – but she knew what I meant about the El Dorado. It hadn't been quite as sleazy last time she was there. Still, never mind. It was all part of our little adventure, she said. We walked around the square for a while, looking at the lights and the posters in the cinema windows.

I bought her an ice cream in a little place in Soho. She said this was a really trendy area now, and the shops were way too expensive. I said she didn't have to tell me, the ice creams had cost six-fifty. She smiled and said she'd give me the money. I told her not to be so silly, but she insisted, so I took it. I gave the waiter a two-quid tip. Well, I didn't want her to think I was mean. She said, 'You only did that because you don't want me to think you're mean.' I tried to be as offended as possible but she just slipped her arm through mine and laughed again, and there was something about her made me want to be happy. So I admitted it and she sighed with mock desperation that men were so transparent.

Catriona was beautiful when she sighed. Wearing jeans and Doc Martens and a Public Enemy T-shirt, she was far more elegant than any of the women we watched swanning out of the opera house in pearls and fur. Her eyes were kind of soft and sparkling, the kind you read about in books. Her face was lightly freckled. She had a way of talking fast and avoiding my eyes that was just irresistible. And she was funny, too. In the wine bar she made sarcastic comments about the posers and yuppies in the corners.

I told her about home and Susan and everything. It's funny how much you can trust and say to a total stranger. And I told her I wasn't really sure what kind of job I was looking for, just something a bit more interesting than sitting in Dublin on the old rock and roll. She said she still had a year to go in art school, then she'd probably come over here and do some course or another. She had lots of friends over here already. In fact, she knew more people over here than she did in Dublin. Lots of people. Bucketloads of them. She'd never be stuck in London, she said.

The thing that got me was this. When we were talking about gigs and holidays and stuff I noticed she said 'we' all the time. We did this. We saw that. Some lucky bastard was obviously going out with her back home, and I suppose she kept dropping this 'we' shit to let me know that. Half-way through the second bottle of wine I plucked up the courage to ask her. She said he was a brilliant guy, Damien, they were really happy together and all that. A really wonderful pass-the-sickbag relationship.

'So, what's happening?' I asked her, pretending not to be jealous as hell. 'I mean, are we talking wedding bells or what?'

'Maybe,' she admitted, 'when he qualifies.'

'And kids and everything?'

'Yeah,' she said. 'I'm sure we'll have children. I mean, why wouldn't we?'

'I don't know,' I said, 'why would you? I mean, why?'

'What is this,' she said, 'twenty fucking questions?'

I suppose I shouldn't have been so pushy and everything. It's not good to pry. I know that, but you know, it was just the booze really. Booze makes some people happy or sad or horny. It makes me curious. Always has. Outside in the rain I felt uneasy and confused. She seemed very quiet now, like there was something on her mind. The mood of things had changed. The feel of the night was suddenly weird and different now. Maybe this hadn't been such a great idea. I told her I was sorry for asking so many personal questions. She just stood there outside the Hippodrome chewing her fingernails and saying nothing.

'Do you want me to go away?' I asked.

She smiled then. She slipped her hand into mine. She said she was sorry too. She didn't know what had come over her. She had things on her mind. She couldn't say. Maybe she'd tell me some other time. She was really sorry, though. Here she was spoiling my first night on London. I told her that was rubbish, and if it wasn't for her I'd be having an awful time. I said come on, here I was in London with a gorgeous woman and not a care in the world. She smiled and looked up at me then. She asked me if I meant the gorgeous bit.

'Yeah,' I said. I did. She said she'd been called beautiful before, but never gorgeous. 'They're not the same thing,' I said, 'not the same thing at all.'

'Charmer,' she said, in a sad voice, 'you're just like Damien.' I said I was sure I wasn't. She said I was, but for one night it didn't matter.

That night Catriona and I made love in the El Dorado Hotel. I had no condoms but she said it was safe. We held each other tight as the bedsprings gave us away. I didn't care. I didn't think about anything except her. I couldn't. Afterwards we lay in each other's arms. I asked her is she sure it was safe. She said yes. Her voice sounded weird. Like she was about to shout. Then I touched her face and she softened. She held my hand very hard.

When I woke up I didn't know where I was. My head hurt and my mouth was numb. She was sitting at the dressing table, putting her earrings in. She said she was going out for the day and wouldn't be back until teatime. She had to see this friend of hers. I asked if it was a guy. She laughed and said no. But she wouldn't let me come. It was just girl talk, she said.

'I'll probably tell her all about you,' she smiled, 'all about how I seduced you.' She kissed me before she slipped out of the room. She said she'd see me back here at eight.

'Yeah,' I said, 'mind yourself.' She said she would.

Down in the breakfast room the Greek grinned lasciviously as he ladled a large sausage onto my plate.

'Eat it all up,' he said. 'You will need all your strength, yes?'

I spent the day dossing around. On Oxford Street the shop windows were full of cheap suits and grim-looking dummies. A guy in sunglasses was selling gold chains from a cardboard box outside the HMV Megastore. 'Any shop in the West End, ladies and gents, they'd costya two hundred nicker straight up but here it's not two hundred, it's not one hundred and fifty, it's not seventy-five or fifty or even thirty. A pony, ladies and gents. First twenty-five pound down gets it.' Nobody moved. 'Come on now, loves,' he said, 'before Mister Plod comes back, who'll give me twenty-five for one of these lovely items?' I walked away and bought a postcard of Princess Diana for my mother. I wrote it over coffee in a little place on Russell Street. I told her I'd arrived safely, and that I was fine, and already making friends. I smiled when I wrote that. I couldn't find a post office open anywhere so I put the card in my pocket and forgot all about it. I never sent it. I still have it in my pocket somewhere, all crumpled up and torn. I've always kept it.

When Catriona came back that night she had an upset stomach. She was bleary-eyed and pale. She told me she'd eaten some awful burger or something, and it hadn't agreed with her at all. I told her to watch it. I told her catching salmonella is the national fucking sport over here. But when she tried to laugh it really creased her up. She had to lie down. She had to get some sleep. Soon as she said that she leaned over and vomited on the floor. I was worried. She walked into the room and flopped onto the bed, shivering and clutching her stomach. She really was in a bad way. When I put my arms around her she started all of a sudden – I mean for absolutely no reason – to cry. I asked her to tell me what was wrong. Had she had some row with her friend? She said, no, she hadn't even seen her. Why not? She snapped at me then. I mean, she nearly bit my fucking head off. She really got weird on me, started saying she had no friends and she was on her own. I said I was her friend and she laughed and said, yeah, things were that bad. Then she said she was sorry. I held her hand as she eased painfully under the sheets, with all her clothes still on. I asked if it was something to do with her period.

'Oh my God,' she sighed, 'spare me the new man bit.' She laughed out loud then, really laughed the bloody roof down. No, she said, if there was one thing it had nothing to do with, it was that. Then she told me she just had to get some sleep. I was to come back and see her later on.

In my room I walked up and down, chain-smoking and flicking ash all over the carpet. I didn't care. Then I lay on my bed and stared out at the lights on the street. What the hell was wrong? Would she be alright? Jesus, say if she bloody died or something. I got up and poured myself a glass of duty free. The tumbler was dirty and it tasted like toothpaste. But I drank it anyway. Then I had another one. Then I had a double. She'd probably be OK. Just some bug or something, that was all. In fact I wasn't feeling so terrific myself. I fed a pound into the television. I watched a documentary about a tribe in the Amazon that eat monkeys.

The bed was wet when I woke up. The stench of the whisky was everywhere. The clock on the wall said ten-past eleven. Shit. I must have dozed off holding the bottle. It was nearly all spilt. My jeans stuck to my legs. I splashed water over my face. I stared in the mirror. I looked awful. My face was pale and my tongue felt all furry. Maybe it was that ice cream we'd had the night before. I don't know. Six-quid-fifty for strawberry-flavoured botulism. Or too much cheap red wine. Yeah. That was probably what was wrong with her. Just a hangover.

When I stumbled in she was sitting up in the bed and wearing my pyjama top. I sat down beside her and asked how she was. She had been crying again. She wrapped her arms around me. The smell of drink filled my head. I told her not to worry. I said everything would be alright. She said my name a few times while I tried to kiss her. She was so beautiful. I couldn't help it.

'Please,' she said, taking my hands off her. She couldn't. It wasn't that she didn't want to. She just couldn't. 'Don't you understand anything?' she said, with tears in her eyes. 'I mean, do I have to paint you a picture?'

I said if she wanted to be like that she could stay on her own. It wasn't my bloody fault she was sick. I told her I bet old Damien wouldn't have stood for this bloody primadonna crap. Who the hell did she think she was, anyway? She told me to get out. I said I was sorry. She started screaming, 'Get out, you shit. Get out of my room.' She picked up a glass and pitched it at me; it smashed on the wall.

When I came back later and knocked on her door there was no answer. I stood in the corridor, apologising through the keyhole. No sound came from the room. The Greek came by and saw me on my knees.

'The ladies, my friend,' he shrugged, 'what can you do with them?' I said nothing.

Next morning Catriona was gone. She'd checked out at seven-thirty, taken all her stuff, ordered a cab for Luton airport. The Greek said he was terribly sorry. I said I hadn't known her that well anyway.

'Still,' he said, 'a very sad situation.' I asked him what he meant. He said no offence, but it was just very sad, a young girl like her.

Breathless, I stood in Catriona's room, staring at the made-up bed and the open windows. My pyjama top lay on the chair by the window. There was a brown bloodstain on it. The Greek's wife came in with an armful of clean white towels.

The young lady had been very ill in the night, she said. They were going to call me but Catriona had insisted that they shouldn't. She begged them not to. She couldn't let anyone find out. If her parents discovered, they would kill her. She explained everything and said it was nothing to worry about. The nurses had told her all this would happen. What she needed now was rest. No worry, and plenty of sleep. It was all over now. But a little discomfort was only to be expected.

The Greek's wife told me she was terribly sorry. She'd thought I would have been aware of things. If only she'd known, she would have broken it more gently. I felt like my whole body was turning to water. She asked me if I wanted a drink. I said no, I still had some duty free left.

I arrived at Aunt Martha's place at lunchtime on Sunday. The door opened and I fell in. She was furious with me. What did I mean, turning up in this drunken state? Did I think this was some kind of boarding house? And where had I been, anyway? She'd phoned Dublin on Friday night to see whether the fog had lifted. My mother had been worried sick about me. I'd better have a good explanation. They were just about to call the police. My father was searching the house for a photo to give them for *The News*. The only one he could find was the one they took the day of my graduation. They didn't know what kind of trouble I was in. Out in the hall I rang home. I said I'd bumped into Johnny Reilly, a guy I once knew in college, who was living over here now. I'd decided to stay a few nights with him. My mother said she wanted me back home on the next plane. She said it was patently obvious that I couldn't be trusted to look after myself.

Alvin and Sharon said it was good to see me. Sharon had purple hair now, and Alvin had a ring through his nose. I managed to croak that I was sorry for all the trouble I'd caused. They shrugged and said not to worry. They said London was all about enjoying yourself. They said I shouldn't let my mother guilt-trip me. In the kitchen someone made me a cup of strong coffee. Alvin said not to pay any attention to Aunt Martha either. He said mothers were all the same. Then Sharon put her arms around me and told me to stop crying. She was sure it would all blow over soon. We'd be laughing about it, she said, in a few weeks.

I went to bed and stared at the ceiling. I wrapped the blanket tight around me. Really tight. Over my head. So tight that it felt like a second skin. And the whole world was shut out now, on the other side of the darkness.

The Wizard of Oz

SO I phoned up Ed and introduced myself. It took ages to get him on the line. This really awful woman kept telling me in her sing-song Cockney voice that he was 'in a meeting' or 'tied-up'. Old Ed seemed to get tied up more often than the Marquis de Sade. But eventually, on the sixth call, he agreed to talk to me. He didn't seem to know who I was at first. Then he said, 'Oh, so it's you, Dave, so you're the wizard of Oz.' This particular joke was one I'd heard about five billion times since I got back – from the old man, my friends, Noreen, everybody, but I had to laugh really. In the circumstances, there was no option. We chatted away for a few minutes and eventually he said, 'OK, listen, Dave, let's do lunch, wait till I get my paws on the old filo.' He told me he had a spare window tomorrow. 'Scruples', he said, a little wine bar, did I know it? I didn't.

That's how I came to be there, in 'Scruples' wine bar on Charing Cross Road, with Ed. I recognised him as soon as he walked in. Like all Irish yuppies, especially the ones that escape to London, he looked slightly uncomfortable in an expensive suit. He looked a bit like he was making his Confirmation or something, you know? He walked over and shook my hand, said, 'Hey, Dave, I knew you'd be the one with the suntan.' He sat down at the table, clicked his fingers at the waiter, said, 'Mein host, por favor.' The second thing I noticed, after the suit, was that he had this terrible grating laugh. I buried my face in the menu, because just about everyone in 'Scruples' was staring at us. It really was a heavy case of beam-me-up, Scotty. Christ, that laugh.

So I said to him, 'Whatever you're having, Ed,' because whatever he wanted to order was fine by me. Then, just in case he got any ideas about who was footing the bill, I said, 'He who pays the piper calls the tune. Right, Ed?'

'Dave,' he said, 'I like your attitude. Absolutely.'

He told the waiter, a little guy with a persistent nervous blink, to bring a bottle of the seventy-five Chablis, real cold, real crisp, and 'a salvo of ham sandwiches all round'. He shovelled handfuls of peanuts into his mouth while we sat there eyeing each other up. I couldn't take my eyes off the poor waiter and his blink. It really was bad. I felt like slapping him right in the face. I just thought one short sharp shock might do the trick.

'Anyway, Dave,' Ed said, 'how is the old sod, and I'm not talking about Charlie Haughey.' I laughed, and told him the old sod was still the same as ever, although I'd only spent a week back there before getting straight on the plane over to London, inflation, cuts, unemployment, all of that. Ed shook his head ruefully while I was speaking. 'Same old story, Rory,' he said, 'same old story.' He told me he'd never regretted coming over here, he'd got out when the going was good, never looked back since he got his ass onto that boat.

I had to listen to fifteen minutes of this, all about Ed's great rise to power, how the Irish were doing very well in England these days, wasn't like the fifties anymore, how he could walk out of his job tomorrow morning just like that and get something else just as highly paid by high noon.

'Advertising, Dave,' he said, 'it's just wide open, man, wide open. It's anybody's ballgame.' The waiter came over and changed the ashtray. He winked. I grinned back at him, wishing I had stayed in bed that morning.

'Anyway,' he goes, 'that's enough about me. Tell me about yourself, guy, what you been doing?' He lit a very long cigarette. I noticed that like a lot of Dubliners over here, for some reason, Ed puts on this slight American accent when he talks.

Let's see. What had I been doing?

'Good question, Ed,' I told him. He did his annoying laugh again. I said I'd been to Sydney, course he knew that, worked in a bar, lots of responsibility, no customers.

'Oh, right,' he went, 'g'day sport.' I laughed. 'Fair dinkum, mate,' he said, 'Charlenes and Sheilas.' I laughed again. 'Koylie Meenowg,' he said. I saw a couple in the corner leaning across the table and whispering to each other. They got up and left.

Before he could get on to the inevitable Crocodile Dundee gags I told him they had a clock on the wall in this bar where I worked with all the cocktails written round the edge. I thought Ed might get a kick out of that. Then I told him about the night me and my cousin drank our way all the way around to quarter-past nine.

He did the laugh and said, 'Get outta here, you're pulling my wire, Dave.'

'No, Ed,' I said, 'I'm not pulling your wire.'

Then I told him about the houseboat and the crazy woman who stole our stuff when we went out. And how I wasn't going with the same girl any more, because she decided to stay over there. Well, I didn't feel like pouring out my heart all over the tablecloth, specially not to Ed.

Ed owns this big place in Docklands, one of those converted warehouses. I suppose he isn't exactly a yuppie.

'Yuppie's such a redundant concept,' he says. What he is is a nipple. New Irish Professional Person in London. Yes, Ed was one hell of a nipple. He was, in fact, the biggest nipple I've ever seen. Foxrock, Blackrock College, Trinity, Progressive Democrats, BMW, doesn't exactly agree with Maggie but my God she's sorted the fucking Unions out, you have to give her that. That's the type of guy he was. He's the kind of guy who says the word 'Yeah' after everything, followed by an ever so slightly inflected '?' So let's run this concept up the flagpole, see if anyone salutes, yeah?

Now you get the picture. And he's also the kind of guy who holds his fingers in the air to make that infuriating inverted commas gesture.

He poured a glass of wine, knocked it back and went 'Cor blimey, kills all known germs dead, yeah?'

He's a friend of my sister, Noreen. They knew each other in Trinity, or 'Trinners' as he calls it. He says Noreen is 'a real sport' and that she's 'easy on the eye'. I think he's got the hots for her, but no point, she's engaged now. My sister Noreen is a bit of an operator, actually, came over to London three years ago, got on the property ladder with the money she got for the accident, bought a place for thirty-two K, just sold it for fifty-three fifty, now she's engaged, for God's sake, *engaged*, with a car, and shares in British Telecom, votes for the Greens because she fancies Jonathan Porrit, against apartheid of course but has to admit she thinks there's too many blacks in London, all of that, and I still haven't even got a damn *job*. Jesus.

When I got back from Oz my mother started nagging me to death. Dad was cool enough but she was just getting tyrannical so I came back over here pretty pronto and Noreen set up this meeting with Ed, to see if Ed could get me a job. Ed is the kind of guy who has a lot of contacts in the City. Or Ed is the kind of guy who *tells* people he has a lot of contacts in the City, quite a different thing.

So this guy with the blink brings the sandwiches over and Ed says, 'Preciate it.' Jesus. You should have seen the sandwiches. Lettuce, parsley, bits of celery, tomatoes cut up to look like rosebuds. The damn plate looked like the Amazon rain forest or something, or what's left of it. And right slap in the middle, kind of nestling, like almost *hiding* under the lettuce leaf, like they were scared, these two minuscule toasted ham sandwiches with the crusts cut off. Mine had a slice of pineapple on the top, and Ed's had a slice of orange, little cherry in the middle, plastic cocktail stick shaped like a sword. Three-Jesus-fifty, the most expensive damn piece of pineapple this side of Carmen Miranda.

He speared my cherry with his cocktail stick.

'Dave,' he said, 'you've just lost your cherry.'

'Right, Ed,' I said, 'good one.' He laughed away at that for a few minutes, wiping his eyes on the serviette. When he threw back his head I noticed that he had hair in his nostrils.

I'm not sure whether you were supposed to eat the pineapple, but I did. In fact I almost ate his orange as well I was so hungry.

'So you like this place, Ed?' I asked.

'Ish,' he nodded, mouth full of parsley. The conversation stopped while he held one hand in the air and tried to swallow. 'It's a bit ho-hum but it's convenient.'

'Yes,' I agreed, knowledgeably, 'it's a bit ho-hum alright.'

'But it's very U, Dave, if you know what I mean.' He held four fingers in the air and made inverted commas again. 'You get me,' he said, 'as opposed to non-U, yeah?'

'Oh, right,' I said. 'I'm with you now.'

Then, all of a sudden, I mean totally out of the blue, of all things, we started talking about this woman, Pamella Bordes, some high-class call girl who was in the news. Ed said, 'Ho ho, Dave, you've come to the right city for that carry-on.' He said for a few quid in Soho, you could have the time of your life.

'Is that right?' I asked. 'So how come you know, Ed?'

'Contacts, Dave,' he said, tapping his nose. '*Vorsprung Durch Technik*, eh?' I told him I thought it was all a bit sexist, actually, and he said, 'Oh yes, Noreen told me you were a bit of a bolshie.' Then he reached across and touched my arm and said, 'Hey, relax, Dave, only pulling your wire.' He went on, 'So hey, Davey, let's talk turkey, Noreen tells me you want to get into the City.'

I said, 'Yeah, Ed, that's the story.'

He went on for a few minutes then about how great Noreen was. That's Noreen for you. Everybody thinks she's so bloody great. They don't actually know the first thing about her, but they all think she's Mother Teresa crossed with Marilyn Monroe or something. Then he said, 'Well, look, Dave, I took the liberty, right, I called this little chumette of mine who runs a rather interesting little unit trust outfit, who as it happens is looking for some willing hands to do a bit of cleaning at the moment, and I mentioned your name, said we were good mates, did the whole business.' He sat back while he was saying all this, with his hands behind his head and a smug look on his face, expecting me to fall down dead with appreciation or something. In fact, I almost gagged on my parsley sprig.

I said, 'Well, thanks, Ed, but cleaning isn't really what I had in mind.'

He said, 'Look Dave, everyone has to start somewhere.' He told me, as if I hadn't heard it a million times from Noreen, all about how Richard Branson started Virgin Records from a telephone box. I mean, he just went on and on, the whole bit, you have to start on the first rung, you name it. So I said, OK, I'd give it a try. Well, he looked so hurt, I had to say that. Noreen would have slaughtered me otherwise.

Then we had coffee. Four pounds for two cappuccinos. I ask you.

'Anyway,' he said, 'got to split, Dave, I'm feeling totally Melvinned.'

'Oh,' I said, 'what does that mean?'

'Melvinned,' he said, correcting himself, 'oh sorry, we have this rhyming slang in the office. Melvyn Bragged, you know. It means shagged. Gas, eh?' I agreed with Ed that it certainly was gas. He had one of those gold credit cards, and that's what he used to pay the bill. He told me to give him a call any time and let him know how things were going. He'd be expecting a few shares when I made my first million.

The next day I lay in bed in Noreen's place until twelve-thirty. Then I phoned Ed's chumette, and she said to come round at ten to clean the office. When I hung up I walked into Noreen and James's bedroom, and had a bit of a snitch around the place, you know, the way you do. Some very interesting reading material in the bedside locker, *very* interesting indeed. I made a mental note to remember all this the next time she tried to nag me. I would blackmail her with the threat of telling my mother. I could just see her face. It's called *The Joy of Sex*, Ma, maybe you should give it a browse.

I hung around the flat all day watching television. I hadn't enough money to go out. I had my Tube fare, and that was it.

I arrived at Jerusalem House at ten-thirty and there was nobody around. I hammered on the glass and eventually this black security guy let me in, locked the door, said his name was Floyd and he'd be down in the basement smoking a joint if I wanted him, which he sincerely hoped I wouldn't. He was wearing tartan slippers. He said to start up on the twenty-second floor.

I pressed the button for the lift, but nothing happened. So I started to walk up the stairs. The building was quiet and cool and everything seemed to be the same shades of matt black and grey and silver. The first two floors seemed to be advertising agencies or something. There were framed posters on the walls. Advertising posters. That guy in the launderette showing off his boxer shorts. Another one for the privatisation of water. Another one with a picture of a soldier with his arms in the air, and words saying, 'This is Labour's Defence Policy; Vote Conservative'. Another one in the same series, long, long queue, 'Labour isn't working'. That reminded me of good old Charlie. Health Cuts hurt the Old, the Sick, the Handicapped. Yeah, Charlie, great. I was looking at that one when suddenly there was a clank and the lift started moving. I missed it on the second floor, sprinted up to Equities National Suisse on the third and just caught it in time.

When I walked into the office I saw this huge open-plan space with maybe thirty desks, all flowing with computer print-outs and pink pages from the *Financial Times*, plants and half-full polystyrene coffee cups everywhere. A light was on in the back office, and a man's jacket was hanging on a chair. But I called out loud and still nobody came. The lights hummed. I called out again.

My heart started to pound. I knew something was going to happen.

I don't know what got into me. I felt weird all of a sudden. I just kind of touched his jacket at first. That's all I wanted to do. Then I took it off the back of the chair and tried it on. I looked at my reflection in the side of a kettle. I turned around and looked at the back of it, over my shoulder. I could feel the sweat on my face. Then, although I tried to pretend I wasn't doing it, I reached slowly into the inside pocket. I really don't know what came over me. His wallet was fat. I took it out and smelt it. Then I opened it, real casually, so that if somebody came in I could say I was just looking for a name and address. Six fifties, five twenties, and more plastic than you'd find in Elizabeth Taylor's face. Jesus. Imagine leaving that much stuff lying around. That guy must have money to burn, he really must. I mean for these people, a couple of hundred is just nothing, small change.

I walked over to the window and stared out over London. Far in the distance I could see the top of Saint Paul's, all lit up with yellow light, a big silly hat on the head of the city. And a cruiser meandering along the river, like a little centipede or something, all made of coloured bulbs. Rain was falling gently against the windows, but they were so thick that you could hear no noise. I imagined I was down on the ground looking up at this black-glass building, with me in the bright window, and all the other lights in the building turned off. London looked like something out of *Star Trek*, all the weird lights flashing, lasers in the sky, reflecting on the river, and the cranes and the concrete walkways all over the place.

I started to tidy round but that damn noise from the lights started to get to me, and I'd no idea which bits of computer print to throw out and which to keep, and anyway I just got fed up. I wasn't feeling well. I walked home to Lewisham in the rain, all the way home, all six miles. I must have seen Pamella Bordes about sixty billion times. When I stopped for the burger they wrapped up my chips in her. Then I saw her again, all over the television shop window, sixteen of her. Then I saw her on a billboard in Peckham. That damn woman just seemed to be everywhere. She was like the Virgin Mary or something, in Ireland. Ubiquitous.

I rang Ed up in his car the next morning.

'Yo, Dave,' he said, 'what's shaking?'

I said, 'Nothing's shaking, Ed, I left the job.' Then he laughed and went 'boom boom', and I laughed too.

Then he said, 'You *are* kidding, aren't you?' and I said, 'No, Ed, I'm not kidding.' There was silence for a few seconds. I could hear the car engine over the crackle of the phone.

He said, 'Look, Dave, I'm having total sense of humour failure on this one.'

I said, 'I'm sorry, Ed, but that building just gave me the creeps.'

'But Dave, you utter Barclays Banker, I went out on a limb.'

'I appreciate that, Ed, I'm sorry.'

'You're *sorry*, whaddayamean, "sorry"? Jesus, Dave, like beam-me-up, Scotty, or what?'

'Can I meet you, Ed?' I said. 'Today or something.'

'Sorry, Dave, no can do.'

'Come on, Ed,' I said, 'give me a break.'

'Time is money, Dave. I can't take time out to help you when you drop me bollock deep in the brown stuff like this.'

I said, 'Come on, Ed, please.' More silence.

'OK, OK, but look, I can't see any blank space until *mañana* at the earliest.'

'Tomorrow's fine, Ed,' I told him. 'And I won't be late.'

Ed said he couldn't give a Castlemaine Four X whether I was late or not, it was my loss. Then he said Jesus Christ again and put the phone down.

By the statue of Eros I sat down in the sunshine. I was tired and still feeling funny. I opened my wallet. I took out six fifties, five twenties, and more plastic than you'd find in a MacDonald's hamburger. And I walked up the side streets of Soho, determined to find myself the good time that Ed had told me about.

Some good time. I went into a peepshow and put a coin in the slot. I saw this woman, maybe about forty, lying on a bed with no clothes on, wearing nothing except a pair of sunglasses. She was reading a paperback novel, *First Among Equals* by Jeffrey Archer. With her other hand, she was smoking a cigarette. The ash on the end was long, and just as she moved to flick it onto the floor it broke off and fell onto her bare stomach. She didn't seem to mind, though. She brushed it out of her navel with the book and turned another page. I noticed she had this thin blue scar across her abdomen. The little cubicle smelt of disinfectant and it made me feel like throwing up. No matter how many pound coins I put in there, I still didn't feel any better. Eventually some dude in a chequered suit came banging on the cubicle door and I had to get out. I went outside and sat on the pavement with my head in my hands.

I spent the rest of the afternoon trying to find a newspaper that had some news about the Irish election. I was wondering whether Charlie was going to get his majority or not, really praying that he wouldn't. I found an *Irish Times* in the end, and I sat in a coffee bar reading the results and lighting one cigarette off the end of another, until it was time to go home.

On the way, I went to Leicester Square Tube station. There was a bit of a commotion outside, this ambulance with a big crowd of people around, four policemen struggling up the deep steps from the Underground with a stretcher. They carried this guy about my age, with a punk-rock haircut and tartan trousers, up the stairs towards the street. A fat man in a uniform was pumping up and down on his chest. He looked more unhealthy than the guy on the stretcher. Every four or five steps they'd stop and heave up and down on his chest again. The fat man kept shouting 'stabilise' and 'release' and 'stabilise' again. They had cut the young guy's shirt open. His chest was tattooed with a crucifix. They carried him right up past me and I saw that his lips were very light blue and his eyes, although they were open, were still and white like a fish's eyes when it's boiled. It reminded me of when we went fishing as kids, down on Dun Laoghaire pier in the summer. That's terrible I know, but sometimes you just think a thing, you can't help it. I mean, what can you do?

James and Noreen took me out to dinner that night, but they were having an argument about the wedding or something, so it was strictly a case of maintaining a tactful silence over the carbonara. I hadn't got a great appetite to tell you the truth.

Next morning I called into Ed's office. I had to wait for about half an hour to see him, in the same room as the woman who answered his phone. She kept offering me coffee, and I kept saying no thanks. She put me sitting on this big black leather armchair that farted every time I moved. She went back to doing the *Telegraph* crossword. Every so often she asked me for help with a clue but I'm useless at those things. Eventually the thing on her desk buzzed and she told me to go in to Mr Murphy's office. On the door were these two little stickers. The first one said 'Ed's Den'. The second one said 'You don't have to be crazy to work here, but it helps'.

Ed was at his desk, holding the telephone between his chin and his shoulder, with one hand over the mouthpiece. He gave me his keys and told me to pop down to the old motor and collect his briefcase for him. He didn't even say hello or anything, just pushed the keys across the desk at me, spun around in his chair and put his feet up on the windowsill.

I walked down to the car park and found his car. The registration number was 'ED M 1'. Noreen had told me he paid £1,500 just to get that registration plate. I opened the door, and the inside smelt new and clean. I saw his briefcase on the passenger seat, but I just sat in there anyway. Just to see what it was like for a minute or two. I clicked on his compact disc player, and Phil Collins came on. That was when I saw his carphone.

I picked it up and dialled Australia. Just like that. I dialled the speaking clock in Australia and I waited for the clicks to give way to the voice. Me and Louise, in all the months we were living together over there, we never got round to buying a clock. So I knew the speaking clock number off by heart. She used to go on at me about how ridiculously expensive it was and tease me because she always had to pay the bill. I sat in the driver's seat just listening to the voice and thinking about her. It was seven o'clock in the evening over there. She was probably just getting ready to go out with that musclebound thug of a boyfriend of hers. I sat there in Ed's car, just listening, for maybe five whole minutes, as the time beeped down the line, until tears started rolling down my face, I still don't really know why.

After a few more minutes I got my head together and dried my eyes on my sleeve. I suppose I just realised there was no point, and that everything she had said about the two of us that night we had too much to drink in the Cantina, it had all been right, pity she had to say it in the way she did I suppose, but still. I was going to put the phone back on the hook, but then I had a thought. It was one of those moments.

I put the phone down carefully, slowly, on the floor, underneath the seat, and I could still hear the voice. I made sure it wasn't disconnected. Then I climbed out, closed all the windows tight, clamped his briefcase under my armpit, locked the door. And as I walked across the car park I stopped, just for a second, to drop Ed's car keys down the drain. I heard him screaming at me, thirteen storeys up. I heard him hammering on the window and screeching my name. I looked up and waved at him. And then, just before I opened his briefcase and slowly emptied its contents all over the car park, I blew him a big kiss.

I walked straight out onto the road and hailed a taxi. I felt light-headed from the tears, stupid I know. Then I said something that I had been wanting to say all my life. The taxi driver's eyes scrutinised me in the mirror. In my mind's eye I saw Ed tumbling down the stairs and shaking with rage. Once again I knew something was about to happen.

'Take me to the airport,' I ordered, 'there isn't a moment to lose.'

Ailsa

I DRANK far too much cheap gin last night. I can feel it all in my stomach now. When I walk around the apartment I can feel it swishing around. I'm feeling pretty damn precarious, I can tell you. I feel like I'm going to do something stupid. It was that cheap stuff, too. That's all you can get around here when you need a shot in a hurry. The guy who runs the shop next door, every time a customer says Jesus, he crosses himself. He's not exactly all there, if you ask me. Toys in the attic.

I've got a feeling in my head that just won't go away. This morning I lay in the bath with my head under the water and I listened to the sound of my breath. My tongue felt like velvet. When I spat in the sink I saw blood. I need to get my damn teeth seen to. Not to mention the rest. Sara made eggs but I just couldn't face them. She said but come on, so I got up and went out for a walk. I didn't even put on my jacket. She gets on my nerves when she gets pushy like that.

It made me have all these weird dreams, too, the gin, and every time I woke up I had to keep real still in case I got sick. Things were crawling over my body. Little things with legs. I was walking through this place in the rain, a park or something, where the trees had wings and I recognised it although when I woke up I couldn't remember. My brain felt like it was wrapped up in cotton wool.

Sara kept looking over at me and asking me if I was OK and I kept saying, yeah, yeah, I'm OK. She grinds her teeth when she's asleep. Sometimes she wakes up laughing. She kept telling me I needed a cup of hot sweet tea. Every time she said those words – hot sweet tea – I felt sick all over again. When I tell her she grinds her teeth, she goes all red and says she doesn't and laughs and tells me to stop kidding around.

At four o'clock this morning I went and sat on the toilet, stark naked with my head in my hands, hiccuping. Then I tried to drink a glass of water back to front but it spilled all over my chest. Cured me though. I sat in the room for a while reading some magazine article about fish or something, I don't know, but it got too cold. I lit a cigarette. Then I lit a match and held it against the tip of another match. The two matches stuck themselves together and I nearly set the damn ashtray on fire. When I got back into bed Sara moved her feet against mine.

A few months ago I fell in love with this woman. She lives down the stairs in the apartment nearest the front door. I don't know why I fell in love with her. I don't think I ever will.

Her name is Caitlin. That's her first name. Caitlin Rourke, funny name. It's a Scottish name, apparently. I looked it up and it's Scottish. Funny, because she isn't Scottish herself. She's from somewhere in America. Even if I didn't know that I could guess. She's just got this faraway thing about her. It's just a feeling. I can't put it into words. She's got long red hair, all down her back. She wears black all the time. I don't know what she's doing living here. But then I don't know what I'm doing living here. Sometimes I really don't. It just happened that way.

I don't know where she works. She's something in public housing or something but that's all I know. She gets this journal. It comes every Friday afternoon. Sometimes, if the weather's bad, it comes Saturday mornings. It's called *Housing Today*. I know because it comes in a clear plastic envelope so you can see the job advertisements on the back cover. There's a lot of jobs in housing, I'll tell you. That's all I know about her, really. And she pays her phone bills late. I know that because I do the same, and you know those little envelopes with the final demand? Well, hers always comes the same day as mine.

Sometimes she leaves her mail down there for days. It piles up. Or maybe she's not always home at night. I wouldn't know. It piles up for days and then suddenly one morning it's gone. I looked her up in the phone book but she's obviously ex. I got a copy of the electoral register in the post office, but it's still in the name of old Mr Johnson and it hasn't been changed yet. Nobody's told them what happened to him. I told the guy behind the counter. He kind of shrugged. Then he said the wheels turn very slowly but I made him take down a few notes just the same. I had to point out that it's people like me pay his wages, the fucking penpusher.

His son came by one day to collect all his old stuff. Old Mr Johnson's son, I mean. He seemed like a nice guy too. Big car full of kids, wife with cross eyes and very blue veins in her legs. They ran up and down the stairs all afternoon and Sara gave them cakes. He rang our doorbell and said he was looking for a Caitlin Rourke. Aren't we all, I thought. Although I didn't say that. Obviously.

One day she got a letter from some guy who signed himself 'Emperor'. What a sap he must have been, signing himself that. His name and address were on the envelope. 'University of Syracuse', it said. Damn intellectual. It was written in pencil. He wrote: I write this in pencil so it's easily erased. Just like me. What a sap. Other times she gets bank statements and stuff and brochures from the book club. And postcards from all over the damn world. She's got these friends who go skiing. The stuff they get up to over there, you wouldn't believe it. And how they put it all on the back of a postcard, when anyone could read it. That postman of ours, he mustn't be too easily shocked.

One morning when I was going out to work I found myself picking up one of her letters. Just like that. I just put it in my pocket. I hated myself later, but that's what I did. I just did it, I don't know, like I couldn't help myself. Walking down to the station I felt really unwell. Then I did it once or twice more, the next week, and then even more often the week after that. Then I did it a lot. Every week. I hate myself, but that's what I do. I open them on the train. I can't help it. See, in our house all the letters get left on this battered old chest that Vera the house loony found out in the back garden all covered in slugs. Vera's got more locks on her door than Fort Knox. She's crazy. She taped a note to the wall. Said: 'Is this anyone's? And if not/so does he/she mind if I use this for the letters?' – little arrow on the note pointing down at the chest. I mean, if anyone had owned it, what the hell was it doing in the back garden?

She's got a good bank balance. Caitlin, I mean. Better than mine, anyway. I started just taking her bills, but then sometimes I take her personal letters too and I open those. I read them in the toilet in the office. I go in there and light up a cigarette and read them. Then I tear them into tiny pieces and flush them away. Sometimes you have to flush twice. People look at me then, like maybe they know, though of course how could they? Sometimes I get this feeling the little bits are going to float back up the toilet or something, and I have to go check. Other times I save them for lunchtime. I read them on the bench in the park, when the weather's nice, eating my sandwiches. I sit there and run my finger through the envelope and unfold the paper real gently and then slowly I read.

One day I tore open one of her letters on the way down to the station and I threw the envelope on the ground. An invitation to a wedding. 'Ms Caitlin Rourke plus one', it said. Nice print too, with gold leaf on the edge. Must have cost a bit. That 'Ms' stuff really freaks me out, though. I have all kinds of arguments with Sara about things like that.

Anyway, I was half way into work when I got this idea that she was going to see the envelope lying on the ground. She would get off the train and walk across the bridge and, just my luck, see the damn thing on the ground. I came all the way back and looked around. The guy in the station asked me was I alright. I really didn't feel too good and it must have shown. It was cold, but my shirt was sticking to my body, and my heart was pumping. It took me an hour to find it and when I got into the office Mr Zimmerman wanted to see me.

She got a real stinker from the book club once, saying payment for her *Collected Dickens* was long overdue and they'd be having to resort to the unpleasantness of legal action soon. I sent them a draft under her name. Another time she got a thing that said if you filled this in you could win a million or a tropical island. You could take your choice. I filled in her name. I wrote 'MISS Caitlin Rourke', and I sent it away. Next day she got a note from the post office, said they understood her husband had reported that her name was missing from the electoral register. I ticked off the boxes and dropped it into the post office myself.

One day I came in and there was a note on the board. 'Someone's been stealing my mail,' it said, 'I would like to know WHO and more to the point I would like to know why. I am REALLY UPSET about this.' Sara said it was awful, and who would do such a thing? She looked up at me, held the phone between her head and her shoulder, took off her slipper, squeezed her foot.

'Probably Vera,' I said, 'you know how she is.'

'Hello,' she said into the receiver, 'is anyone there?'

I went into the kitchen and splashed water on my face. Sara was speaking very slowly, the way people do with those answering machines.

At ten o'clock she stood up and said, 'I'm going to bed.'

'Go to bed,' I told her, 'I will be in soon.'

'OK,' she said, 'if you're going soon, I'll wait for you.'

I told her, 'Sara, for crying out loud.' She went to bed.

I've never said a single word to Caitlin Rourke. Once or twice we've met on the stairs, but always she just turns away. She has a long straight back. She looks kind of capable, like some women do. Like she wouldn't let you down. She looks like nothing could shock her. I've seen her down in the station too, getting off the same train, but she always lags behind so she won't have to talk to me. She stops and reads the timetables, that kind of thing. What's she reading the damn timetables for? I mean, she gets the same damn train every day.

One day I climbed the stairs behind her, looking up at her long black-stockinged legs. She gets the same train every day. I told you that, didn't I? Other times, she's fiddling with her keys in the doorway when I'm walking up the road. I pass by the gate and go get some cigarettes or, like last night, some gin. There've been house meetings but I've always got Sara to go. I couldn't stand it. Being in the same room as her would just kill me. I'd fall to pieces. As if things aren't bad enough.

One night Sara came back up and told me a funny story about Vera and something she said to Caitlin at the house meeting. I asked her if Caitlin had a boyfriend or anything. I had just finished doing the dishes and the skin on my hands was all wrinkled. I said has she got a boyfriend? I knew she wasn't married. Sara goes why? Are you interested?

That was our first really bad argument. It got out of hand, I admit it. I know she didn't mean it, but lately I've been feeling funny about stuff like that. I'm not myself any more, not since Mr Zimmerman let me go. It's all the sitting around. It just doesn't suit me.

I had to drive her to the hospital that night. We told the doctor she fell down the stairs. I wasn't sure if he believed us. She wanted me to see someone but I promised it would never happen again. I swore it wouldn't. That night she laughed in her sleep too. I couldn't bear to look at her the next morning, with her face like that. I asked her if she would be back tonight and she said she didn't know. Then she said she'd nowhere else to go, and she started to cry. I phoned her at the office at lunchtime and things were a little better. I promised it would never happen again. I said I don't know what's wrong with me. I think I have been working too hard. She said what do you mean working? and I said looking. Never mind, kid, she said, you'll find something soon. She calls me 'kid' sometimes. She told me that things would get better for both of us soon. She said you have to have a bit of belief in your life. I told her I loved her but she couldn't talk. Yeah, she said, I do too.

Sometimes in the night I get up and go for a walk. I don't sleep too easily. I stand outside her door in the dark, just listening, to see if I can hear anything. I stand there on the landing. Then I go down to the tracks and watch the night trains going by. I wonder where they all go to. You think the whole world is asleep but the trains just keep rolling. I stand on the bridge and look down. I spit over the side. It's cold down there, but you can see things more clearly. You hear the tracks kind of whining long before a train comes.

Sometimes when I'm here during the day I want to smash down her door and break her apartment to bits. I want to go into her bathroom and turn on all the water and let it soak through the floor. I want to take off all my clothes and lie between her smooth cold sheets. I want to search through her stuff. I want to take off my clothes and walk around her apartment. I want to open all her secret drawers.

One day I rang her bell. Then I rang every other bell in the house, but everyone was out so I was safe. I came back upstairs and tried my key in her lock. It didn't work. Thank God, I suppose.

A few months ago was the last time I saw her. She'd put on a little weight. She was looking so good, I almost said something to her. She buried her head in a magazine and when we got to our stop she didn't get off even though I knew that she had seen me. I stood on the platform and watched the train pull away. She never looked up but I knew alright.

It was Christmas, actually. I remember she said to Sara we should come down for a drink. I said I have a headache, you go. She said how come you always have a headache when people invite us. I told her she could go by herself. I said we didn't have to do every single damn thing together. I said you're getting too dependent. She said this morning she's too independent, now she's too dependent, she just can't win with me. That's it, I told her, turn it all into a game. She didn't go. She went down with a bottle of wine and said we had to go to Handel's 'Messiah' with this friend of her sister's.

She told me that Caitlin had put on a little weight. Oh, I said, has she, and what other news have you got if you're such a big deal. She said it's obvious the counsellor is doing you no good at all and I said, for God's sake, I'm warning you, don't start all that again.

That was Christmas, like I said. Last week I came in and there was another note. 'Caitlin and I have a baby girl!!' it said – 'and her name is Ailsa.' Signed by someone called Tony. Blue paper. Cheap.

I stood in the hall for a long time, just looking. Then I went upstairs. Sara didn't know who he was, but she said wasn't it so nice of him to write that, all the same. A lot of men wouldn't, she said. A lot of men are out of touch with their emotions. There were tears in her eyes when she said it. She went all quiet. She said it was just the onions in the casserole. There were tears in mine, too. Then she said it was just her hormones. She hugged me tight and told me she'd never realised I was so sentimental. It was a few days later when I found out she'd stopped taking the pill. Then she suggested we send a card, congratulations, just leave it downstairs on the dresser for her, with all her other mail. I said no. Yes, she said, that will be something for you to do. I said no, but she said yes, you know how you're supposed to take responsibility for things.

I lay in the bath this morning with my head under the water. I listened to my breathing and to the beat of my heart. I lay there perfectly still until the grey water went cold all around me.

Phantom

I'M SITTING in the front room of Jimmy Strange's house on a hot night in August. The birds are awake, croaking with the heat. It's already getting late, but the sky is still bright, and we're all feeling good.

The TV is on in the corner, but the sound is turned down. It makes everything in the room look blue.

I'm here with Jimmy, and my wife Maria, and Jimmy's new girlfriend Coral. She's a lot younger than him. Nineteen maybe. We're eating salami and peanuts. We're laughing. Charlie Parker is on the stereo. Coral is pregnant. She really shouldn't be having such a good time, or so she keeps telling us. Motherhood isn't about having a good time, she says.

When she laughs she throws back her head and howls. You can see right down her throat. You can see the fillings in her teeth. But we like her, Maria and me. She's good for Jimmy, even though she's a little crazy. We're inside, and it's night, but Coral is wearing sunglasses. She's one hell of a talker. She's told us fifteen times how happy she is to meet us. And we're happy to meet her too, at last, after this two years and all the stuff about her in Jimmy's letters. We're all friends here. We haven't seen Jimmy for such a long time. We've come home to Dublin for a few days, just to say hello. It's good to see him looking so well. He's put on a little weight. He says it's in sympathy with Coral and he laughs. He's happy.

We've been drinking for maybe ten hours. All the beer is gone, but we're drunk so we want more. There's a big black plastic sack of cans on the floor. Jimmy says the room looks like an office in the Australian Embassy. I want to go buy some more but Maria says I shouldn't drive in this state and anyway all the shops are closed. It's Sunday. So we start into a dusty bottle of some green stuff that Jimmy and Coral picked up in Greece last year. I can't remember what it's called. Tastes like peppermint to me. Peppermint and nothing more. Coral says it tastes of sunshine. She says it reminds her of how much they were in love then. She throws back her head, and she laughs like that's just the funniest thing she's ever heard. Maria laughs too. Then they quieten down, catch each other's eyes, suddenly crease up laughing again. They seem to get along fine, the two of them. They seem to understand each other without speaking. The way some women do.

'Everything was closed that night in Mykonos,' she giggles, 'everything was closed, so we went home and made this baby.'

Jimmy doesn't laugh. He smiles, but looks a little uncomfortable.

Jimmy must be thirty-five now, because I am thirty-three. We've known each other all our lives. We grew up on the same street, and we were in the army together, out in Lebanon. Peacekeeping. That's a good one. But he didn't save my life or anything, we're just friends. Maria and I have seen Jimmy through a lot, his marriage breaking up, his child being taken away from him, other hardships too. We knew his wife Sheila well, but we don't talk about that any more. With Jimmy, that's a touchy subject.

They get on well. Maria and Jimmy, I mean. They always have. They like each other, although they're very different. That's nice for me. It makes things easier.

When Jimmy and Maria are out of the room, Coral wants to know all about us. How we three got to meet. I'm drunk. She's insistent. I talk too much.

I tell her that when we were younger, before we got married, Maria and me split up for a little while, and she and Jimmy took up together. Coral laughs and says that's typical. I tell her to say nothing, because I know Jimmy's funny about it. He thinks I don't really know all the details, but of course I do. Maria and me try not to have secrets.

Still, it just shows you. That's how close we're talking here. If things had been different, I tell her, it could have been Maria and Jimmy. Coral says Maria is lucky, and I laugh and say I know.

'So you got back together then,' she says, 'you couldn't keep away?'

So I say yes, we started going out again, and Maria got pregnant. I tell Coral that wasn't the only reason, but we got married a couple of months later, and I've never regretted it. Maria's the only worthwhile thing that ever happened to me. Coral says, 'Ah', she thinks that's really sweet. And I say that we've been very lucky together.

'And the baby?' she says.

'Well,' I say, 'I'm afraid we lost it, just after the wedding.'

'Lost it?' she says, and I tell her I don't mean literally lost it. I mean it died, before it was born. I'm drunk you see.

I agree that it's sad, and it was hard for us. But I don't want to dwell on it, not with her in this condition. I'm stupid about things like that. I tell her Jimmy was great at the time. I tell her that's when you know your real friends, at a time like that.

Jimmy comes in with Maria. She's carrying a plate of sandwiches. He's carrying the icebucket. He says a lot of water's been passed between us three, that's for sure. He's right too.

'He's just told me all this really nice stuff about you,' Coral says.

Maria sits down beside me. She says I must be drunk. She looks beautiful. Coral thinks we have a marriage made in heaven. Maria says she doesn't know about that. Purgatory maybe. She always says that, but I don't mind. I know she means it nicely.

Coral stands up. She looks a little unsteady. She's wearing a green smock. She's so small she looks like this baby's just taken her over. She pulls off her sunglasses and polishes them on the tablecloth. Her eyes are bleary. She says we should go sit in the garden, so we pick up drinks and bottles and cigarettes and go. It's darker now. The moon is red. Coral says it looks like a bullethole in the sky. She starts to giggle. Jimmy is getting a little uptight, but he does that sometimes.

She puts her arm around his shoulders. She has to stand on tiptoe to do that. She ruffles his hair. He blushes. It's nice.

'Don't worry, petal,' she laughs, 'I won't make a show of you.' She's slurring her words.

We're talking about the old days. We're talking about all the people who've gone away now. We think it's sad, the way people have to go away from here to do anything. Jimmy says we just don't care in this country. We treat people like sheep, then we're surprised when they bleat. Coral laughs at that.

'Baaa,' she goes, 'baaa,' then she holds her hands to her nose and laughs again. Suddenly she stands up. She comes round the table and holds Maria's face in her hands. She tells Maria she should be a model. 'You have bone structure, and when you have that, you're always beautiful.' She kisses Maria's mouth. Then she comes to me and she does the same thing. She smells of beer and cigarettes, but that's a smell I don't mind. She holds my chin. She tells me I'm beautiful too. I tell her there's no accounting for taste.

'She's right,' Maria tells me, 'you *are* beautiful.' Everybody laughs. Everybody except Coral.

'What are you laughing at?' she pouts. 'He *is* beautiful.'

'Hell, we're all beautiful,' says Jimmy, 'it's like Mr and Mrs Universe here.'

'*Ms*,' says Maria, 'please.'

Jimmy makes a face.

'It's so good to have friends like you,' Coral says, and she pats her stomach. 'I think this baby'll be the luckiest baby in the world.'

Maria laughs, but she looks a little upset. She has that look in her eye. We can't have babies now, her and me. It's not her fault, although fault is apparently not a word you should use. We just can't. There is something wrong with my vas deferens, and there doesn't seem to be much we can do. God knows, we've tried. My vas deferens has been put through some stuff. I could tell you horror stories.

It wasn't always there, this problem. Obviously. But it's there now, and it just won't go away. Funny, really. When we were young we spent all our time trying not to get pregnant, and we did. Now we *want* to get pregnant, and we can't. Typical. I know she is thinking about this. I'm her husband. I may be drunk, but I understand the way she thinks.

So we've been sitting there in the garden for a while, laughing, talking, when suddenly things seem to change. I know the reason. Maria goes quiet, starts staring up at the trees. She takes a match, starts chewing it. I know what's on her mind, but I don't want to make an issue of anything.

'Do you think we'll always be friends?' Coral says. She looks very serious now. She takes a slug from the green bottle.

'Course they do, stupid,' laughs Jimmy, 'what are you talking about?'

He's getting very drunk now. We all are. Suddenly I'm aware of it.

Coral closes her eyes. When she speaks, she shakes her head from side to side. She waves her arms in the air. She has bangles around her wrists.

'I'm talking about *friends*,' she says, 'I think these people are wonderful. I love them. I'd hate to think we won't ever know them.'

'You hardly even know them now,' he says, 'that's crazy pregnant talk.'

'We'll be friends,' I say, 'don't you worry, Coral. I've been through too much with this bastard.'

'Of course we will, Coral,' says Maria, 'don't you worry.'

The way she talks to people, it makes me want to put my arms around her.

'When I think,' Coral says, 'I knew people before. I thought they were my friends, now I hardly know them. They don't speak to me since I took up with Jimmy.'

'Why is that?' Maria says.

'Because he's already married, I suppose,' she says.

'Their loss,' Maria says.

'Yes,' I agree, 'hypocrisy is easy.'

It isn't really what I mean to say. But everybody agrees anyway.

'You're always on about this crap,' Jimmy tells her, 'you worry too much about people.'

Coral sits down beside him and kisses his neck. 'I know you're right, lover,' she smiles, 'you are right. I know that.'

And then, a few seconds later, a weird thing. Out of the blue, Maria puts her hands to her face and starts to cry.

I'm shocked, believe me. I don't know what's happening now. It isn't the baby stuff. That never makes her cry. But I don't know what it is.

'What's the matter, Maria?' Coral says. 'What's wrong?'

'Yes, love,' I say, 'what's the matter with you?'

'I was just thinking of something in the past,' she says, 'my dad and a friend of his. He was talking about it again when we saw him yesterday.'

Coral looks a little sick. She twists her hair around her fingers. She stares at Maria.

'What's so sad?' says Coral. 'What's to make you cry in that?'

Maria looks up at her. She wipes her eyes. She looks awful now.

'It's nothing,' she says, 'but you made me think about it just for a second, what you said. About friends.'

'Tell us,' says Coral.

'No,' says Maria, 'it's really nothing.'

'Beam-me-up, Scotty,' I think, 'not this one again.'

'Tell us what happened,' says Coral, 'we're *your* friends, you can tell us.'

Maria says it's a long story. She doesn't want to bore us all to death. But Coral insists. She says a problem shared is a problem halved. She says she wants to help. I know what my wife is going to say now, but I say nothing myself. This always happens when Maria is drunk. She's very sentimental. She thinks about the past too much. Always this story too.

She gathers her breath and begins to speak.

'This was a friend of my dad's when he was in the police,' she says. 'His name was Michael Fahey. We called him Uncle Mike. When my mother died, he used to come to our house a lot. Him and my Dad were the best of friends.' She looks at me. She raises her eyebrows. I give her a tissue. 'You met him once or twice, Pete, didn't you?' she says to me.

'Yes,' I say, 'he was a nice man.'

'He was famous,' she says, and then she laughs. 'He was the man who caught The Phantom.'

'Who's that?' says Coral. She's trying to catch peanuts in her mouth. Maria laughs again, and she blows her nose.

'Oh, he was just some crook, you know, in Dublin in the sixties. He was a burglar. He had these stupid printed cards with this stupid name, The Phantom. He left them in the houses that he burgled. The newpapers loved it. It was before your time, Coral. It was a big thing back then. It was the sixties, you know, not much else was happening.'

Jimmy laughs. 'Yeah,' he says, 'not in this country, anyway.'

I look at Coral. Her eyes are bright and curious. She pulls on her cigarette, leans back her head. She blows smoke rings into the air.

She looks like a child herself. She looks too young to be anyone's mother. For some reason, right then, I feel very sorry for her.

•

'And then,' says Maria, 'one day in 1968, my Uncle Mike Fahey found him. In a church somewhere. Nobody knew how he did it, but when he came out of that church he had The Phantom in handcuffs.'

'Wow,' says Coral. '*Wow.*'

'Yes,' laughs Maria, 'really something. He drove him back to the station and my dad signed the arrest papers.'

'Cool,' sighs Coral, 'so what happened then, Maria?'

Maria laughs again. She looks happier now. She picks up a glass. She drinks some of the green stuff. She shudders.

'To The Phantom? He got seven years. But Uncle Mike was a hero. His picture was in all the newspapers. He got promoted. People used to stop him in the street to shake his hand.'

'A bishop sent him a letter of congratulations,' I say, 'isn't that right?'

'Yes,' she giggles, 'that was funny.'

'So this guy was a superstar,' Coral laughs, 'right?'

'Yes, he was,' laughs Maria, 'in a way. We used to boast about him in school. And my dad was so proud too. He was never jealous. Nothing like that. He used to cut articles from the papers about Uncle Mike. He kept them all in a scrapbook somewhere.'

'Oh,' says Coral, and her eyes are dreamy with drink. 'I wish I had a famous friend in the newspapers.'

Maria is plucking at the edge of the tissue paper.

'Yes,' she smiles, 'they were good friends.'

'So?' says Coral. 'So what happened to them?' Maria sits up straight. She's picking at her fingernails. She's holding her wedding ring, turning it, round and round. 'Did they fight, was that it?'

'No,' says Maria, 'that wasn't what happened.' Maria sighs. She starts to speak. She speaks quietly, like she doesn't want someone to overhear. 'Uncle Mike started drinking,' she says, 'just like that, for no reason that anybody could see.' She sighs again, and she shakes her head. 'That's where it all went wrong. He just turned up at the station one day, with the smell of whiskey on his breath. After a while, that started happening all the time. Something took him over, I suppose, the way it does with some people. It was something he had in him.'

'Same old story,' Jimmy sighs. 'Just like my dad.'

Coral laughs, suddenly. Then she puts her hand to her mouth and goes red.

'I'm sorry,' she says, 'I always laugh when I hear sad things.'

Maria looks at her. 'That's alright,' she says, 'I do that too.' I'm tired now. It's late. Really, I want to be at home, in bed with my wife. 'He started to forget things,' Maria goes on, 'just not to care about things anymore. And a funny thing, he started to curse. His appearance changed too. His face. It started to look rough. He smelt. He put on a lot of weight,' she says, 'here and here,' pointing to her stomach and her neck.

'Did he stop coming to your house?' Coral asks.

'No, no,' says Maria. 'Sometimes he slept on the couch in our front room. I remember walking in one morning, and that horrible smell, you know? That smell of a drunk sleeping it off.'

'That's a smell I know,' Coral giggles, then she puts one finger to her mouth and whispers, 'Only joking.'

Jimmy looks angry. 'So what happened then?' he says, lighting a cigarette.

'Well, people tried to give him advice,' Maria says. 'My dad gave him the name of some doctor.' Then, suddenly, my wife's face wrinkles up. Tears come to her eyes. Her voice cracks when she speaks. I can't stand to see her like this. I feel so helpless. 'But none of it was any use, something just took hold of him. It was a terrible thing to see.'

Maria is crying like a baby now. Her mascara is running down her cheeks. There is silence, apart from her sobbing. She keeps saying she's sorry.

'It's just a love affair,' Jimmy sighs, 'us Irish and drink, it's like a fucking marriage or something.' He pours himself another glass.

'Oh shut up, Jimmy,' says Coral. She too is about to cry. She crawls over to where Maria is sitting. She holds Maria's hand. Maria looks at her face. She strokes it. She wipes away her tears.

'Then,' Maria says, 'I remember the night everything went too far. I think I was nineteen.'

'I think we've talked enough about this,' says Jimmy.

'Shut up, you,' says Coral, 'just be quiet.'

Somewhere in the distance I can hear the sound of bottles breaking.

'I think you were there, Jimmy,' Maria says, gently, 'I think you were in our house that night.'

Jimmy looks at me. He laughs. Then he glances at Maria.

'No I wasn't,' he says.

'You were,' she says, without looking, 'don't you re-member?'

He stares at me again. He shakes his head.

'I don't remember that,' he says, 'honest Indian.'

Then he looks at Maria once more. He pulls a face. He scratches his head. But Maria isn't looking at him. She's looking at Coral.

'Yes,' Maria says, 'Jimmy was there alright.'

'I think maybe I was just passing,' he says, 'and I called in.' He's looking at me now. 'I think that might be it.' He sounds nervous.

'He's sweet, isn't he?' says Coral.

'Yes,' I say, 'he is.'

'Oh yeah,' Jimmy says, very quickly. He snaps his fingers. 'I remember now. I was just passing the house.'

'One in the morning,' Maria says, 'and the phone rings in the hall.' Jimmy starts staring into his glass. He rattles it a little. I can hear the ice cubes. 'Yes, it gave us a fright. When my dad came down to answer it, it was the station.'

'Your dad was in bed?' I say. 'When the phone rang that night?'

She looks at me, like she doesn't know what I'm talking about.

'Yes,' she says, 'of course. It was late, he was in bed.'

Jimmy coughs.

'Maria's dad looked worried *that* night,' he tells me, 'I remember it now. He stood in the hall, kind of running his hands through his hair, going, oh Jesus, oh my God.' He looks at me and he nods. 'It's coming back to me now,' he says.

'Yes,' I say, 'that's something you'd remember alright.'

'I asked him what was up,' Jimmy says. 'He said it was big, big trouble. He walked up and down the hall for a while. Then he took his handcuffs or something, didn't he, Maria, and he drove into the city.'

She nodded. 'In his pyjamas,' she says, 'he didn't even change into his uniform.'

'What was the matter?' Coral says. She's sucking at the crushed ice through a straw.

'I really don't know what happened exactly,' Maria sighs, 'but it was something that some guy who'd stolen a handbag had been choked to death in the back of a police car. Something about a struggle, and somewhere Uncle Mike was involved. My dad tried to do his best. But it couldn't go on any more. That's how it was put. My dad cried when he came home.'

'You should have seen it, Pete,' Jimmy says, and he clicks his tongue. 'It really was something terrible, when you're that age, to see a man like that cry.'

I say nothing. His eyes look afraid.

'I suppose I just forgot about it,' he shrugs. 'It was such a long time ago now.'

'That can happen,' I say.

'So what happened to poor Uncle Mike?' says Coral.

'He lost his job,' says Maria, 'just like that.'

'The bastards,' says Coral.

Maria nods. She crushes out her cigarette, very slowly on the path. She looks a little nervous now.

'I'm sorry,' she says, 'I'm sorry about this . . .'

My wife stops speaking. She gnaws her lip. Coral hands her a cigarette and she takes it, lights it up. The flame makes her face orange.

Jimmy is scratching his head again. 'Christ, it's weird,' he says, 'the way your memory plays tricks with you like that.'

'Then Uncle Mike went to England,' my wife says. 'He had a brother there. But he had to move away from his brother's house too. There was a quarrel, just a small family thing, but it had got out of hand. I suppose when people are drinking, that's what happens.'

'Oh yeah,' says Jimmy. 'It is.'

'Yes,' she nods, 'he moved on somewhere. He just disappeared for a while. Then one day he wrote to my dad, to say he'd been offered some job, working for some burglar-alarm company, with his own office, his own secretary, all of that.' Her eyes fill up with tears again. Her voice shivers when she speaks. 'He was going to straighten himself out and make something of his life. He was going to stop drinking, try to get something back. He wanted to be friends with my dad again.' I reach out to touch her hand. Her fingers close around mine, but she doesn't look at me. Coral is holding her other hand. She looks up at me and smiles. Maria is trembling now. She speaks again. 'Then one Christmas, my dad wanted to go over and visit him. He telephoned Uncle Mike's brother in England. The story about the new job, the burglar alarms, that was all a lie. Uncle Mike was sleeping rough in Manchester. That was all his brother knew.'

'Oh my God,' says Coral.

'Dad got a list from the station library and he wrote to every hostel in Manchester. But there was no word. He put notices into the newspapers over there. But nobody knew where he was. He'd just disappeared again.'

'What happened to him, Maria,' says Jimmy, quietly, 'in the end?'

Maria looks Jimmy in the eye. She looks like she's accusing him, although, of course, she is not.

'They found him seven months later,' she says, 'in London. They pulled him out of the river. He was naked.'

Maria bends her face into her hands. Her shoulders begin to shake. She cries once more. I touch her.

'Don't,' I say, but it does no good. She's breathing in and out, very hard.

'You see, my dad left it too late,' she cries, 'it broke his heart. He was never the same after all that. He missed him so much, you see, they shared so much of life together.' She bends over and cries into her knees. Her hands are in her hair.

'You just reminded me of it, Coral, I'm sorry.' She opens her mouth and sobs. Her face looks like she's in pain.

Coral is kneeling. She bends forward. She is holding her stomach.

'I think we've had enough,' I say, 'I don't think we want any more of this story.' I take her head and bring it to my shoulder. She cries, and I touch her hair. She's my wife. I want to take care of her. Jimmy is looking at me all the time. When I look back at him, he smiles. Then he looks away. Up at the trees.

The time passes.

*

It's very late now. Jimmy and me are still sitting in the garden. Coral is inside being sick again, and Maria is looking after her. She keeps coming out here to get a handful of ice cubes, then going back inside. Jimmy is quiet. There is something on his mind.

There is silence in the garden. It's broken only by the sound of the distant traffic, up on the dual carriageway. For some time we don't speak. My jaw feels heavy. I look up at the sky. I hear the sound of Coral throwing up. Jimmy closes his eyes.

'Not again,' he sighs.

The clouds are pink and red. The air is clear. A plane is going in front of the moon. It looks black. I wonder where it's going.

Jimmy picks up an empty beer can and crushes it in his hand.

The sky is getting bright now. Dirty yellow light is spreading across the garden. I'm feeling too drunk to talk. I watch Jimmy rolling up another joint. I ask him if he has heard from Sheila. I know I shouldn't, but I can think of nothing else to say. He tells me his ex-wife has gone away to California. She's living with a cousin. The cousin is divorced.

'She writes to me about all this crap,' he says bitterly, 'all these guys and stuff. Fucking surfers, you know?' He shakes the bottle of green stuff. He laughs. 'I'll tell you, man,' he sniggers, 'she's giving a new meaning to the phrase bed and board.'

'Well,' I say, 'now you're happy with Coral.'

'Oh sure,' he shrugs, 'happy. That's not everything.'

'Maybe you should've thought of that,' I tell him.

'Oh, thank you,' he says, 'thanks for the input.'

Then there is silence for another few moments. Jimmy drags on his joint, nodding, staring at me, giggling. He picked up a taste for that stuff when we were in Lebanon. I have no time for it myself.

'Bitch,' he says. Just that. Suddenly he stands up. He's rocking on his feet. His eyes are watery. I don't think he really knows where he is. He glares at his watch. 'Come on,' he says, 'I have an idea. Let's call her up and say hello.'

'What?' I say. 'You're crazy.'

'Yeah. Let's call Sheila up and see how's her fucking karma.'

'I have to go, Jimmy, it's way too late.'

'No way,' he insists, grabbing me by the arm, 'she'd love to hear from *you*, man. We all know that.'

'No,' I say, 'I don't want to do that, Jimmy.'

Jimmy looks at me like we're not friends at all. He lets go of my arm. He pushes me in the chest. He grins at me. He keeps blinking.

'You're so fucking mature,' he says. 'Victor fucking Mature. You've never made a mistake in your life, have you?'

'I've made mistakes,' I say. My voice is hoarse.

He pushes me in the chest again.

'No, no, you haven't,' he says, 'you're perfect, aren't you?'

'Don't start,' I tell him. I can't stand up straight now. My knees are shaking.

'I'm warning you, Jimmy,' I say, 'just don't start anything.' He grabs my shirt, and pulls me towards him. I feel his breath on my face. 'Let me go, Jimmy, please.'

'It's really good to see you, man,' he slurs, 'we should keep in touch more, you know?' He throws his arms around my neck, and pulls me tight to his chest. He slaps my back. He kisses my cheek. 'Fucking loyalty is a great thing, don't you think?'

'I really have to go,' I say, 'Maria's getting tired.'

Jimmy pulls away from me. He crushes out his cigarette against the wall.

'Does she get tired easy,' he says, 'these days?' He grins at me. I start to straighten my tie. My face feels hot.

'I have to go,' I say, 'where's my keys?'

He clears his throat. He reaches out a hand to steady himself against the garden seat. He laughs loud. Then he holds up his hands. Like someone has just pointed a gun at him and he's going to surrender.

'Pete, Pete, Pete,' he sighs, 'relax, man. You're too uptight.'

I look him in the eye.

'Fuck you, Jimmy,' I say, 'you'll never change.' My voice comes out louder than I want it to. Wind blows in the leaves.

He stares at me suddenly, like he doesn't even know who I am.

'I hope not, Pete,' he says. 'I'll leave all that to you.'

'Now what's the problem here?' says Maria. When I turn, she's standing behind me. She walks out of the shadow with the moon on her face. She looks better now. She's rubbing her hands together, drying them off. Her hair is tied back. She has a white towel around her neck. She looks beautiful.

'Here she is, folks,' says Jimmy, 'now *here* is one hell of a woman.' He picks up an empty glass and holds it in the air. 'Just saying, Maria, that Pete here is a lucky man.'

'Oh please,' sighs Maria, 'don't start all that. Come on Pete, get the keys, it's late.'

*

Jimmy opens the front door and stares out at the sky. He looks like he has never seen the dawn before in his life.

'So you're really going?' he says.

'Yes,' she tells him. 'We really are.'

He looks down at his feet. 'Well, take care of Victor fucking Mature here,' he says.

'You're drunk,' she tells him, 'you should be looking after Coral.'

'That one's a survivor,' he says, 'anyway, you're drunk too.'

'No,' she says, 'I'm sober now, Jimmy.'

'Oh fine, fine,' he says, as though he couldn't care less. 'Beautiful. You're sober.' I know that he is looking at me, even though my back is turned. 'So, when are you two bastards going back to London?'

'Tomorrow,' I say, though this is not the truth.

'Yes,' she says, immediately, 'first thing tomorrow.'

'Tomorrow,' he says, 'that soon?'

'Some of us have to work for a living,' I say.

Jimmy laughs. 'Beautiful,' he says. I hear the ice cubes tinkle in his glass once more. 'Well, I wish we'd see you again, but if you have to go, I suppose there's nothing I can do about it.' I turn. He holds his hand out to me, and I take it.

His handshake is wet. His head is bowed. He does not look at my eyes. 'Don't forget to stay in touch,' he mumbles. 'That'd be nice for Coral.'

'We won't forget,' says Maria.

She steps up to him. She kisses him quickly on the face. He runs his fingers over her hair. He tries to hold her. She pulls away. She takes my hand. He pretends not to notice.

'See you next time you're over?' he says. 'Please? Don't forget?'

I button up my jacket and look at my watch. It's twenty-past six.

'We'll be in touch,' Maria says, 'but we really have to go now.'

We walk down the steps. We sit into my sister's car and I start it up. Maria wipes the inside of the windscreen with her fingers. She says nothing.

The morning is suddenly very cold. The birds are singing like crazy now. They've been awake all night. They sound angry. We pull out slowly onto the road. I see Jimmy Strange in the mirror. He is standing on the steps behind us. He is waving.

'Please don't forget,' he shouts. I watch him, just for a second. Maria puts her hand on my thigh. She tells me she loves me. 'Don't forget,' Jimmy roars, 'for Christ's sake!'

All the dogs start to bark. I put my foot down. Hard. I feel the tyres biting into the gravel.

Glass Houses

THAT MORNING, Fred Murray stood on the porch in his 'Italia 90' T-shirt, sweating already, though he was barely out of the cold bath. He stared up at the sky. He shook his head. He crushed out his cigarette on the gravel.

'Not a cloud in sight,' he sighed, 'it's going to be another killer.' He took his wife's face in his hands, and kissed her lips. She yawned, and pulled the belt of her dressing gown tighter. 'Ninety-nine degrees, the radio said that's what we'll hit today.'

'Maybe you'd cut that grass this weekend,' she said, 'the heat's dried it out and I'm worried.'

'Why?' he said. 'What's the worry?'

'Those kids around here,' she said, 'they have nothing to do in weather like this. One match and the whole house could go up.'

'They're only kids, Anne,' he said, 'it's summertime.'

Fred Murray looked at his wife. Her eyes were nervous. She was chewing her fingernails again. She knew it drove him crazy, but she did it anyway. She kept chewing, until the nails were gnawed down to the fingertips, and the soft flesh behind them was exposed and bleeding.

'Let's go out again tonight,' he said, 'let's take a drive up to the mountains. It's cooler out there.'

'I have my unislim at eight,' she said, 'and I've already taken a goulash out of the freezer.'

'We can leave it,' he said, 'that doesn't matter.'

'Not on the money you bring home we can't,' she said.

'I can't help that,' he told her, 'people don't want taxis in this weather.' Fred Murray looked at his wife's face. It was thin and white. 'They don't want taxis, Anne,' he repeated,

'I'm worn out trying.'

'I just wish it would rain,' she sighed, 'I'd love to lie in bed and listen to the rain.'

'I have to go,' he said.

'I know you do,' she nodded. 'See you later, Fred.'

With one click of the key the engine started. Fred Murray pumped the accelerator. He listened to the engine roar. It felt good to be taking off for another day's work. He had to admit it. He did not even know what might happen. Or who he might meet. But it felt good all the same.

He drove to the end of the road. Mr Milligan was kneeling by the flowerbed in his front garden. He had a radio on the lawn beside him. He took off his hat. He waved it in the air, at Fred Murray. Fred Murray gave him a thumbs-up sign. He honked his horn.

Fred Murray drove slowly through the avenues, out towards the edge of the estate. He drove down the hill towards the turning for the main drag into the city. The heat was already unbearable. Sweat dripped from Fred Murray's hands and his face. It dribbled down the steering wheel. It ran down his back and in between his legs.

He pulled up at the junction. He craned his neck to see. There was nothing coming. Fred Murray pulled his sunglasses down over his eyes. He flicked on his radio and swung onto the grey dual carriageway. He licked the sweat from his upper lip.

Hitting fifty, the wind whistled through the open windows and Fred Murray felt better. He tuned the dial on the radio. He turned the volume up loud.

> 'I'm walking on sunshine,' sang the radio,
> 'Oh, oh, I'm walking on sunshine,
> Oh oh, I'm walking on sunshine
> And don't it feel good . . .'

And Fred Murray sang along, at the top of his voice.

The girl in the petrol station was very pretty. Her skin was freckled, and she had the reddest lips. She was wearing a pair of blue shorts and a Lou Reed T-shirt. Fred Murray took his change and went back to the car. He started up the engine. He saw that the girl was staring at him. He eased out onto the road, waving at the girl through his window. She laughed, but she didn't wave back. Fred Murray threw his free stamps into the glove compartment.

He thought about his wife again. He'd found her in the bathroom late one night, staring at her face in the mirror, crying.

'Come in, thirty-seven,' said the control, 'Fred, something for you, in the Berkeley Court Hotel, if you want it. Name of Hutchins.'

'Ten four, Frank,' said Fred Murray, 'I'm on my way now.'

'It's some bigshot, Fred. Going mad in the heat. Make sure you're there on time, alright?'

'I said I'm on my way, Frank,' sighed Fred Murray.

He flicked off his FOR HIRE sign, turned left, sped around the block, past the school where children screamed in the yard. Then he started back on the road for the Berkeley Court.

He was just thinking about his wife. He was thinking of the look in her eye on the night he had found her there in the bathroom, crying, when the young woman stepped out from behind a parked bread van and into the path of his taxi.

It seemed like a long time before the car struck her. Her face got bigger and bigger in Fred Murray's eyes. He could see her hands, thrust towards him. He could see her blue eyes clearly. And her open mouth. He stood on the brake. He spun his wheel hard. His head hit the ceiling of the cab. His hands were so sweaty they slipped off the wheel. He grabbed it again. He could smell burning rubber in the air. His tyres screamed. The car bucked from side to side.

The young woman tried to dodge. Fred Murray opened his mouth, but no sound came.

The car shuddered as the side panel caught her. It made a horrible *thud* sound. She did not fall. She stood very straight as she grazed against the side windows. Then the back fender caught her on the thigh. The force sent her spinning across the street, back into the path of the oncoming truck. Her legs tangled. She fell to her knees, then over on her side.

Fred Murray heard screams. An old man on the pavement dropped his shopping bags. He put both hands to the side of his head. Fred Murray managed to stop his car. He looked over his shoulder, out through the passenger window. His heart pounded. He saw the young woman lying in the middle of the road, with her hands stretched out towards the truck. She was barefoot. Her stockings were red. She was yelling, 'No, no!'

Black smoke poured from the wheelwells of the truck. The driver's face looked white. His eyes were wide, as the truck bore down on the young woman.

'Oh my God,' said Fred Murray. But somehow the truck stopped, just a few feet before where she was lying. The engine cut out, and a high pitched whirring sound came from under the bonnet. The driver leaned over his wheel with his head in his hands. A line of cars behind started honking their horns. Shopkeepers ran out from their premises. A butcher came, knife in hand, blood all over his apron. The truck driver leaned out his window, and started waving his fist at the cars behind him. 'Shit,' said Fred Murray, 'thank you, God.'

When Fred Murray got out of his car, the young woman was lying on her back in the middle of the street. Her yellow blouse was ripped all down one sleeve, from the shoulder to the cuff. She was crying. She had blood in her long blonde hair, and smeared across her mouth. A middle-aged woman and a thin-lipped, middle-aged man were leaning over her, poking at her ribs. The middle-aged man was holding a pair of women's shoes. One of the heels was broken off, and his wife was holding that. They belonged to the young woman, he said, as Fred Murray came over.

'You stepped out in front of me,' Fred Murray said, 'are you alright?'

'Get his number, Frank,' hissed the middle-aged woman, as though she did not want Fred Murray to hear. 'They all have a number on the inside of their cabs, go get it, quick.'

The middle-aged man stared at the sky. He began to whistle. He walked past Fred Murray, and towards Fred Murray's taxi, staring, all the time, at the sky. Fred Murray said nothing. Several cars had stopped now. They had just stopped dead in the middle of the street, and long lines of traffic were building up.

'That's him,' somebody said, pointing at Fred Murray, 'that's the guy that hit her.'

Fred Murray leaned over the young woman and touched her arm. His shirt stuck to his flesh. He felt the sun on the back of his neck.

'Do you feel any pain?' he said to her.

'I'm alright,' she cried, 'I'm sorry, I didn't see you.'

'No,' said Fred Murray, 'I didn't see *you*.'

The young woman lay up on her elbows. She looked up at the faces around her. A boy gave Fred Murray a bottle of lemonade. Fred Murray held the young woman's chin and poured some of the liquid down her throat. She spluttered. She looked at the faces again.

'Get lost,' she said, 'I'm not going to die. There's nothing for you to see here.' Nobody moved.

'You heard her,' snapped Fred Murray. 'You're not helping things one bit.'

People began to drift away, all except for the middle-aged woman, who kept glaring at her watch, then at her husband. Her husband was still peering nervously through the window of Fred Murray's cab.

'Do it,' she hissed at him, 'for God's sake, can't you do *anything*?' She took an envelope from her handbag, looked at her watch. She began to write some words on the envelope.

The traffic started to move again. The truck driver stared down on the group of people in the road as he pulled slowly past. He shook his head when he saw Fred Murray. He smiled sarcastically, and shook his head from side to side.

The young woman had stopped crying now. Her face was cut and grimy, and she had lost a tooth. Fred Murray dabbed at her lips with a handkerchief. His fingers were sweaty. He felt like vomiting. His heart pounded. He wanted to lie down in a cold, dark room.

'I'm really terribly sorry about this,' said Fred Murray.

'Please,' said the young woman, 'don't upset yourself.'

'So you should be upset,' said the middle-aged woman, 'driving like that. You're a professional driver. Didn't you ever hear of the rules of the road?'

'I've been driving seven years,' said Fred Murray, 'this has never happened to me before, swear to God, not once.'

The young woman sat up. She leaned her head forward, between her knees. Fred Murray touched her hair. Then she sat up straight and wiped her eyes. She blinked in the hot light.

'That's alright,' she croaked, 'I think I'm going to be alright now.'

'You're a menace,' said the middle-aged woman, to Fred Murray. 'You're a danger to yourself and everyone else too.'

In the corner of his eye, Fred Murray saw the middle-aged man slowly open the back door of his cab and lean in. He stood up straight. He held his hands to the sides of his mouth.

'That vehicle is private property,' shouted Fred Murray. 'You touch it again, I'll be forced to have you prosecuted.'

'Don't you talk to my husband like that,' said the middle-aged woman. 'People in glass houses shouldn't throw stones.' Fred Murray ignored her.

'Away from that car now,' he shouted, 'I'm warning you, pal. I mean it.'

The man blushed. He closed the back door of the car and walked away from it, hands thrust into his pockets, back towards his wife. Fred Murray got down on his knees in the road, and he took the young woman's hand. He stroked it. He told her to relax.

'You should loosen up your shirt,' he said, 'that'll help you breathe.'

He reached out and opened the top two buttons of her shirt. She stared at his hands. He wiped his forehead.

'What are you doing?' said the middle-aged woman, 'you're going to make things worse, touching her like that. I'll call the police.'

'I have my first-aid certificate,' snapped Fred Murray. 'Just because I'm a taxi driver doesn't mean I don't know anything.'

'I'm fine, I'm fine,' sighed the young woman, 'I just want to get up.' She held her hand over her eyes and looked into Fred Murray's face. 'Would you mind?' she said. 'I don't feel too solid.'

Fred put one strong arm around the young woman's waist. She put her hands on his shoulders. He put his other arm behind her knees. He lifted her to her feet. She stood up straight, smoothed the front of her skirt. Her face was red. She looked around for her shoes, and the middle-aged woman handed them to her. The young woman coughed, turned her head, spat on the road. Then she leaned her hand against the lamp post to support herself. Her face looked white now. Her stockings had been ripped at the knee, and the inside of her right thigh. Her skin showed through the holes. A black bruise went down her right cheek. The palms of her hands were grazed and bloody.

Fred Murray took the first-aid box from his back seat. He held the young woman's fingers and poured disinfectant on her hands. She shuddered, and dug her nails into his wrist.

He cut a length of gauze, and made bandages.

'That's better,' she whimpered, 'I feel better now.'

'Let me take you to a hospital,' said Fred Murray. 'Just for a check-up.'

'No, no,' said the young woman, 'I don't like hospitals.'

'Well, let me take you to a doctor, then,' he said. 'It's the least I can do.'

'I don't need a doctor,' she said.

'I feel just terrible about this,' said Fred Murray. 'I've been driving for seven years, and this has never happened to me before.'

'You won't be driving another seven,' said the middle-aged woman, 'when we report this, you'll be finished.' Fred Murray said nothing. He put his finger on the young woman's pulse, and he stared at his watch. 'What's your name, please? I need it for my complaint.'

'Now look,' said Fred Murray, 'why don't you just mind your own business?' The woman turned to her husband.

'Are you going to let him talk to me like that?' she said.

'No,' he said, 'don't talk to her like that.'

Fred Murray stared at the man. He smiled.

'I'm shaking,' said Fred Murray. 'I'm really terrified now.'

'There's no need to be sarcastic,' the man said. Fred Murray turned away.

'Your pulse is OK,' he said, 'are you sure you don't need a lift?'

The young woman looked at him. She rubbed the back of her neck. She stared at the ground, then back at Fred Murray's eyes.

'Well, you could take me to my mother's house,' she said, 'she lives over on the northside. I was planning to go see her today.' Fred Murray glanced at the middle-aged woman. She looked angry. Her eyes were narrow, and her breasts moved up and down when she breathed. She folded her arms and glared at him. 'I mean, if you really mean it,' continued the young woman, 'if you're sure.'

'Yeah, yeah, I'm sure,' said Fred Murray, 'it's the least I can do.' He went to his car and picked up the radio. 'Six-five, Frank, can you send somebody else for that BC job? I've run into something here.'

'What,' said the control, 'you're not *there* yet? Jesus, Fred.'

Fred Murray looked at the young woman. She was holding a mirror to her face, brushing her cheeks with powder. She pulled her shirt out of her skirt. She stepped into her broken shoes.

'I don't know, Frank. It's the heat. I think my radiator's gone.'

'Fred, Fred, I told him you'd be there twenty minutes ago.'

Fred Murray felt his anger rise.

'Alright, Frank. I'm lying to you, alright? I'm really fine, I'm actually trying to put you out of business. I just think that's why God put me on this earth, to make your life as miserable as possible, Frank. Well done, Frank, you caught me out.'

'OK, OK, Fred,' said the radio, 'I just hope she's good looking.'

'Typical,' said Fred Murray, 'you're disgusting, Frank. You think with your dick, you really do.'

Fred Murray's hands shook as he turned the steering wheel. The backs of his legs were damp with sweat. He reversed out onto the road, only noticing then that his side mirror was missing. He looked at the young woman. She wiped her forehead with the back of her hand.

'Where'd you say?' he asked.

'St John's Road,' she said, 'do you know it?'

''Course I know it,' snapped Fred Murray, 'I'm a taxi driver.'

'Sorry,' she said. 'I didn't mean to offend you.'

'No,' sighed Fred Murray, '*I'm* sorry. It's this heat.'

'This is a nice taxi,' she said, 'is it new?'

'Well, it's new second-hand,' he said, 'I just got it last month.'

'Yes,' she said, 'it smells new. That's a nice smell, a new car.' Her fingers touched the dashboard.

'My wife cleans it for me,' he said, 'she does it every few days.'

'That's good of her,' said the young woman.

'Yes,' said Fred Murray, 'it is.' And then there was silence.

'Fabulous weather,' she said.

'Oh yes,' said Fred Murray, 'tremendous.'

The young woman began to cough again. She spluttered and slapped her chest with her hand, until tears filled her eyes.

'Listen, really,' said Fred Murray, slowing down, 'I think we should see a doctor.'

'I told you,' she said, 'there's nothing wrong with me. I just swallowed something the wrong way. Have you got a tissue?'

Fred Murray opened his glove compartment and pulled out a packet of tissues. He watched as the young woman wiped her eyes.

'I don't suppose you'd like to stop somewhere for a drink,' he said, 'just to pep you up?'

'No thank you' she said, 'I'm pregnant.'

'That's nice,' said Fred Murray.

'Yes,' said the young woman, 'I suppose it is.'

Then there was silence. The young woman stared out at the passing streets, leaning her elbow in the open window, closing her eyes against the wind. When Fred Murray went to put on the radio, she asked him to leave it off.

'I've been driving this taxi for seven years, you know,' he told her, 'I never had an accident yet.'

'Look, please don't worry about it,' she said, 'I'm not going to sue you.'

'I don't know what I was thinking of,' he said, 'I really don't.'

'You must be in love,' the young woman said.

'No, no, no,' laughed Fred Murray, 'not me. I've been married fifteen years.'

'You can be in love and married too,' she said.

'That's not what I meant,' said Fred Murray, 'I know that.' The young woman laughed. 'So what's your husband do?'

'Oh, I'm not married,' said the young woman, 'not just now.' Fred Murray nodded.

'Great,' he said. She laughed again, and fanned her face with her hand. 'So what about your baby, if you don't mind me asking?'

'I do mind you asking,' she said, 'I don't want to talk about that.'

For the rest of the journey, they didn't talk much. The young woman looked tired. She said she wanted to sleep. Fred Murray left her alone, and she began to doze in the passenger seat. Beads of sweat covered her forehead. She lay back in the seat, shifting, trying to get comfortable. Her skirt rode up around her thighs. Her hands lay folded across her stomach. She breathed in deeply. She began to snore.

Fred Murray looked at her. She was young enough to be his daughter.

He took the most direct route he knew, speeding out into the suburbs on the northside. When he passed another taxi driver on the road Fred Murray waved, or flashed his lights. That made him feel good. It made him feel that he was not alone. And when he came to St John's Road he pulled up, coughed gently, and touched the young woman on the knee.

'We're here,' he said. The young woman lay very still. 'We're here,' said Fred Murray, nudging her again. She didn't move. Fred Murray touched the back of her hand. She still didn't move. He heard the sound of his own breath. Very gently, he lifted her arm. It felt heavy. 'I said we're here, wake up.' The young woman's face was white. Fred

Murray looked at her chest. She didn't seem to be breathing. Fred Murray started to get nervous. 'Come on, love, I can't hang around here.' She lay still. He lifted her arm again, and dropped it into her lap. Sweat poured from Fred Murray's face. 'Are you alright?' He touched the girl's forehead. He poked her thigh. He did it again. He held her forearm and shook her, gently.

Suddenly the girl's head fell forward and thumped against the dashboard.

'Fuck,' said Fred Murray.

He held her shoulders and sat her up in the seat. Her legs were slightly parted. Her head nodded again. He pushed it back. This time it stayed. Fred Murray lifted the young woman's blonde hair out of her face, and pushed it behind her ears. His jeans felt soaked through. Her arms fell down by her side.

Fred Murray looked up and down the street. Nobody was coming. He touched the girl's eyelids. They stayed closed. He forced them open. Her eyes were wide, staring. When he took his fingers away, they closed. He slapped her cheeks. Her head nodded to one side. Her mouth opened. Her tongue lolled out the side of her mouth.

'Oh my God,' said Fred Murray. He touched her tongue. He tried to take it between his fingers and push it through her lips. He tried to lift her head again, but it kept falling. 'Oh Christ.'

Fred Murray sat still. He stared at the girl, at the top buttons of her shirt, the soft part of her neck. He looked out the window. Then he stared at her face again.

Fred Murray could hear his heart. He felt cold now. He stared at the young woman's knees. At her thighs. He rubbed his palms on his shirt.

Suddenly, a black car sped past his window.

Fred Murray's temples throbbed. He looked up and down the road again. He wiped the sweat off the back of his neck. He couldn't breathe properly. He made sure nothing was coming. He reached out slowly, very slowly, towards the buttons of her shirt. He couldn't stop himself. His fingers were shaking.

'Boo!' she yelled.

Fred Murray's heart skipped a beat. The girl sat up straight and began to laugh. She lowered the sunguard and looked at her face. She combed her hair with her fingers. She held her hands to her nose and shook with laughter.

'Oh my God,' said Fred Murray.

'I'm sorry,' she giggled, 'I thought I'd just give you a fright.' Fred Murray touched his chest.

'You did that,' he said, 'you certainly did that.'

'I'm sorry,' she said, 'I'm always doing that. Pretending I've kicked it. I shouldn't have done it to you, though.'

'No, no,' laughed Fred Murray, 'I'm just glad. I mean, that you're alive after all.'

'Yes,' she said, 'could have been very embarrassing for you.' She looked him in the eye. 'A corpse in your car.' She smiled. 'All that.'

'Well, there nearly was one,' he said, 'it was nearly me.'

'Oh, I'm sorry,' she laughed, 'I really am.'

'Hey, forget it,' laughed Fred Murray, 'I'm OK, believe me.'

But Fred Murray didn't feel well at all. When the young woman had got out of his car, he drove around the city for a while, with the radio unplugged and his FOR HIRE sign off. He pulled into a garage and got a can of coca cola from a vending machine. It tasted sweet and warm in his mouth. It made him want to spit. He wiped his lips with the back of his hand. He felt the heat on his scalp.

'Don't you have any cold drinks?' he called to the boy at the till.

'No,' he said, 'sorry. The heat's made the refrigeration pack up.'

'Jesus,' said Fred Murray, 'a day like this and you have no cold drinks.'

'Yeah, well,' shrugged the boy, and he began to whistle, stacking chocolate bars onto the shelf by the till. 'What can I do?'

'Typical,' snapped Fred Murray, 'that's just a beautiful attitude.'

Fred Murray pulled a coin from his jeans and went to the phone booth. He stuck the coin in the slot and dialled his home number. It was busy.

He sat outside the car wash with his legs apart and his head down between his knees. When he looked up, he watched the huge purple nylon brushes swish across the windscreens, seeming to devour the cars. His legs felt weak. A car full of nuns went through the car wash. When it came out, the nuns stared at him.

He went to the call box again. His shirt was wet through now. His eyes itched. When he touched his face, it felt hot. The sun looked white in the sky. He burnt his hand when he touched the paintwork on the wall.

He tried his home again, but the number was still busy.

'Shit,' said Fred Murray, 'shit, shit, shit.'

He sat down again. He felt faint. When he tried to stand up, his legs felt like rubber. He stood in the bathroom, splashing cold water over his face. Then he tried the number again.

'Anne,' he said, 'it's me.'

'Fred,' his wife laughed, 'this *is* a surprise.' She sounded nervous.

'Anne, it's just . . .'

'Oh, I'm so glad you rang, Fred,' his wife said, suddenly, in a very loud voice. 'I meant to say, Fred, would you get me a bottle of brandy, while you're out? I want to make a start on the Christmas cake.'

'Is there somebody there?' he said.

'No, Fred,' she said. She laughed. 'Why?'

'I thought I heard a voice.'

'No,' she said, 'just the TV, Fred. I'm watching something.'

'It sounded like a person,' he said, 'not the TV.'

A young woman in tight jeans and a black vest eased out of a little car and walked across the court, clutching her keys. Her back was tanned. Fred Murray could see it, above the neckline of her vest. Fred Murray watched her walk. She knocked on the office door, turned towards the sun, wiped her forehead, turned back, stepped into the office.

'So what about that brandy, Fred?' his wife said. 'I'll need a whole bottle.'

'For Christ's sake, Anne,' he groaned, '*Christmas cake*? It's July.'

'I know that, Fred,' she laughed, 'these things take time.'

'Can't you get it yourself?' he said. 'I'm supposed to be working.'

'Well, no, I can't,' she said, 'you know I can't go down to that shopping centre, with all those kids around, Fred. I thought you'd know about my nerves by now. Just hold on. I'll turn the TV down.'

Fred Murray said nothing. He put one finger in his ear, to drown out the traffic. He listened, carefully.

He watched the young woman walk out of the office, and back to her car. Just before she got in, she held the hem of her vest in both hands and shook it. Then she dipped her fingers in the water bucket. She ran her hands up and down her arms. Then she opened the car door and slid into the driver's seat. Fred Murray turned away.

'So what are you watching,' he said, 'what's on the TV?'

'Fred Murray,' she laughed, nervously, 'is there something on your mind?'

'No,' said Fred Murray, 'nothing at all.'

'So why are you ringing me in the middle of the day,' she laughed, 'checking up? Do you think I'm having an affair or something?'

'No,' he said, 'that's not what I thought at all.'

'No,' she said, 'that's good, Fred Murray. Because I'm not.'

'I know that,' he said. 'Neither am I.'

His wife laughed, as though what he had said was ridiculous.

'Is it hot out?' she said. 'Somebody told me it would hit a hundred today.'

'No,' said Fred Murray, 'it's hot, but it's only ninety-nine.'

'That's not what I heard,' said his wife. 'A hundred. Someone said that.'

'Who?' said Fred Murray.

'Oh,' she said, 'just someone on the TV.' She laughed again.

'No,' he said, 'it's only ninety-nine, Anne. I just checked.'

'Anyone can make a mistake,' she said. 'But I won't keep you, Fred. I'll let you go now. I'm sure you're very busy.'

'Yes,' he said, 'I am. Goodbye, Anne.'

When he had hung up, Fred Murray walked to the edge of the station forecourt. He sat down on the rail, on the edge of the dual carriageway. He felt the sunburn across his forehead. He watched the cars whizz past for a while. Then he stood up and walked to the edge of the road. He looked out to his left, as far as he could see.

On the grass islands of the motorway, groups of workmen were slashing at the grass with scythes. They had taken off their shirts. Their backs looked red. All down the motorway, as far as he could see, lay huge piles of freshly cut grass. The heat made everything shimmer.

And the smell of the newly mown grass was intoxicating to him, sweet in his head like some kind of drug.

Fred Murray sat down. He lit a cigarette. He found himself wondering why that smell made him feel so uneasy, and if it was possible to turn such an unspeakable thing into words.

The Long Way Home

RAY PRIEST came tiptoeing down the stairs at ten to midnight on the thirty-first of March and he walked out the front door to his car. Very gently he turned the key and the engine began to hum. He looked up at the window of the room where he had left his wife sleeping. He hesitated just for a moment, and then he pulled out from the kerb.

Ray Priest didn't know where he was going that night. But he knew he was going somewhere, and he knew he wouldn't be coming back. For weeks now, since their last big fight, he had been moving his clothes and his papers out of the house, a little at a time, stacking them up in cardboard boxes in his brother's garage.

At twelve-fifteen his brother was waiting in the garden, with a flashlight, as they had arranged. He looked cold in his tartan dressing gown. Ray Priest got out of the car. He looked up at the sky and said the forecast was for heavy rain.

'Jesus, I don't know about this, Ray,' his brother said, 'can't you give it one more go? I don't like to think of you running off in the middle of the night like this.'

'Shut up, Frank,' said Ray Priest.

'You're forty years old,' said his brother, 'you're a grown man.'

'And you're my brother,' said Ray, as though it was an accusation.

'I'm your brother,' he said, 'but that doesn't mean I have to like it.'

'I told you already,' said Ray Priest, 'everything's over with Maria and me.'

'But how do you know, Ray?' said his brother. 'Give it one more shot, just for me, please?'

'I'm sorry, Frank,' said Ray Priest, 'but my shooting days are over with that woman.'

They loaded the boxes into the back seat of the car, and then his brother sighed, and they shook hands under the streetlight. Ray Priest heard dogs barking. His brother asked him where he was going, and Ray Priest said he didn't really know yet, but he'd be just fine. He'd be in touch as soon as things had settled down a little.

'It's better this way,' said Ray, 'it'll hurt her less.'

'Man, I don't know,' said his brother, and he scratched his head. 'She'll kill me, Ray, if she ever hears about this.'

'She won't hear,' said Ray, 'if you don't tell Anne.'

'Are you kidding?' asked his brother. 'I think one broken marriage is enough for this family.'

Ray Priest drove until the lights of the city were behind him. He came down onto the dual carriageway at Dolphins Barn and he swung out onto the open road, by the canal. He felt better now. He felt so good that he surprised himself. Speeding through Clondalkin he flicked the radio onto a country music channel. Every song seemed to be about broken promises, so he changed to the World Service. Things were looking bad in Liberia, they said, it might be war any day now. He turned off the radio, rummaged in his glove box for a cassette, and put on Waylon Jennings singing 'Blue Suede Shoes'.

He sat up straight in his seat, with his hands locked on the wheel. He thought about what would happen next morning when his wife would wake up and find that he was gone. She would be upset, he knew that. But after all this time, and all these arguments, they would be better off. He knew that too. They were destroying each other, not to mention the kids. He couldn't bear their life together any more. And neither could she. Sometimes, he told himself, you have to be cruel to be kind.

The dual carriageway was wide and empty, flanked on both sides by the racing fields and stud farms of the Curragh. A strong wind was blowing up and it made the car shake a little at the high speeds. The night was white and hazy. He would miss her, that was for sure. But something in their lives together had just disappeared now, and there was nothing more they could do. They had to face that much. He tried to stay alert by counting the horse boxes, all lined up against the white rails by the road. But after a while, the scenery grew dull, and flat. Ray Priest opened his eyes wide and blew air through his lips.

Passing Rathcoole, he began to feel tired. The road was too straight and the blur of the yellow helium lights all down the way was hurting his eyes. And the road was lonely too, with only the overnight truckers and the tape machine for company. Drizzle speckled his windscreen. He watched a police car come speeding towards him in the opposite lane, heading towards Dublin, with its blue light flashing. Then he pulled off the carriageway and drove up the tiny uphill roads into a little town called Clane. He parked outside the fire station, and he went to get a hamburger and a black coffee in a tiny joint that was still open on the main street.

He sat on the window ledge looking out at the clouds, and trying to make sense of the crumpled map. Behind the counter a young girl with red lipstick was listening to a walkman, bopping her head from side to side in time to the music. A cigarette hung from her lip. Lightning ripped down the sky. Thunder cracked over Clane. Rain came hammering down against the chip shop window. Ray Priest sat looking at the coinbox telephone while he chewed slowly at his hamburger and sipped his bitter coffee.

Rain was falling hard now. Gusts of wind blew litter through the streets. A dustbin overturned with a crashing sound, spilling its contents into the wind. Ray Priest sat in his car for a minute, thinking. He flicked on his wipers, double speed.

'Oh boy, oh boy,' crooned the DJ, in a warm and husky voice, 'that's going to be a wet one tonight, people. Now that's a night for shutting out the world, and smooching on down with the one you love.'

Ray Priest pulled up his collar and lit a cigarette. He started up the engine and pulled away, down through the main street of Clane, taking the side road that went south, and avoided the dual carriageway. A little scenery would do him the world of good, he thought.

Ray Priest drove on, through the towns of Rathangan and Kildare and Monasterevin and Old Lee, and the green dark spaces between them. He sped past abandoned thatched cottages with their walls beaten in, castles brooding in the fields, dancehalls with broken shutters and corrugated roofs. Coming into Portarlington he slowed down to a crawl. He looked at the pink flashing light in the hotel window. 'WELCOME TO PORTARLINGTON', it said. 'NO VACANCIES'.

This was a town he knew. He remembered the night that he and his wife had stayed in that hotel, after her sister's wedding. He remembered the way his wife had looked at him that evening, the way they had danced together in the red ballroom, and the way the crazy light from the mirrorball had shone in her dark hair.

He stopped outside the hotel and stared up at the windows. He listened to the rumble of thunder, and he wondered what might be going in that hotel, right now – if only it was made of glass, and he could see right in. Then he moved on again, through the town, past The Dublin Bar and Mick Manley's Pub, slowly over the bridge at the other side. The river was churning now, white with froth underneath the bridge. Ray Priest felt alone.

He wondered where he was going. He stared down at the foaming water, then he eased into first again, and began to drive once more.

Then suddenly, in the still of the road, Ray Priest saw something move. Out of the shadows by the gate of the Protestant church stepped a young man in a leather jacket. Ray Priest swerved. The young man had a rucksack, which he held tight to his body, and long black hair, straggly with rain. He stared at Ray Priest's car, with a hopeful look. He stuck his thumb in the air, and jabbed it up and down.

Ray Priest drove straight past him, feeling a little guilty. But twenty yards later he slowed down, thinking what the hell, maybe it might be nice to have some company on his journey.

Ray Priest stopped and he flashed his emergency lights. In the mirror he watched the man pick up his bags and run towards him. Rain seemed to roar in his ears. He pushed open the passenger door and looked at the young man's shiny pink face. Wind screamed across the bog, rattling the flagpoles in the church grounds.

'Where are you going?' said Ray Priest. Thunder boomed. He had to shout, to be heard above the sound of the storm.

The young man's face was thin, and his skin looked unhealthy. His nose was a little crooked. He had a black scar across his upper lip, and his eyes were bright. Lightning crackled.

'Anywhere,' laughed the young man, 'you name it.'

'I'm thinking of Cork,' said Ray Priest, and the young man said Cork would be just fine. He sat into the passenger seat, dripping all over the floor.

'Good Christ,' he said, and he sniffed. He wiped his face with the back of his sleeve and he pulled out a pack of cigarettes, looking at Ray Priest with a question in his eyes. Ray Priest could feel the cold from the young man's body. As the car began to move, he noticed a tattoo on his passenger's wrist, shaped like a Spanish dancer.

'Go ahead,' said Ray Priest, 'the ashtray's in the door.'

The match flared. Ray Priest smelled sulphur. The young man's fingers shivered as he lit his cigarette. His nails were dirty.

'Whore of a night,' said the young man. He sounded like a local.

Ray Priest said it looked like it would get worse before it would get better. The young man nodded, but he appeared to be far away in his mind and thinking about something. He pulled on his cigarette and did not speak.

'So,' said Ray Priest, 'what are you running away from?' The young man looked at him.

'Oh, I'm running away from reality,' he said, and he laughed.

'Yeah?' said Ray Priest. 'I'm just running away from the wife.'

'Oh,' said the young man, 'why are you doing that?'

'That's a long story,' said Ray Priest, and he felt himself blush. He glanced at the young man. 'I'm just kidding you,' he said. 'I'm not doing that. Not really.'

'No, you're not kidding,' said the young man, 'what about all that stuff in the back there?' Ray Priest smiled.

'Holiday,' he said, 'I'm going to see my brother.'

'She know you're going?' said the young man.

'Who?' said Ray Priest.

'Mother Teresa,' said the young man. 'Who did you think? Your wife, of course.'

'Oh yeah, oh yeah,' said Ray Priest. 'Her idea.'

'I see,' said the young man, 'her idea.'

'Oh yes,' said Ray Priest, 'I mean if it was up to me I'd stay at home, but, you know, it isn't. My brother is very sick. He had a heart attack. I don't want to talk about that too much.'

The young man said he was sorry to hear it. He began to whistle through a gap in his front teeth, and to drum his fingers on the dashboard.

'Sickness is a terrible thing,' he said, and he shook his head from side to side, running his fingers through his long wet hair.

They drove on in silence for some minutes. The towns got smaller and the lights more infrequent, and after a time Ray Priest began to wish that he had not stopped after all. Something about this silent young man gave him a bad feeling.

'Terrible about Liberia,' the young man said suddenly, and Ray Priest agreed that things were not looking good. But the young man did not answer him. He just stared straight through the windscreen, nodding, whistling through his teeth, saying nothing at all.

'So what about you?' said Ray, eventually. 'What's your story?'

Ray Priest tried to sound interested. It was not that he really wanted to know anything about this young man. It was just that he did not want to sit in silence, feeling edgy, all the way to Cork.

The young man said that he was looking for work. He had just got engaged to a girl from Mullingar. They had been going together for a year, and they planned to get married the following September, live with her father for a while, then get a place of their own. The girl did not get on too well with her father. But they had no money just now. The young man had no work, and his girlfriend had just been made redundant from her job at the factory, and she was having trouble finding something else. So the young man was travelling south, to find some work, and see if his luck would change.

'It's kind of late to start hitching now, isn't it?' said Ray.

The young man had taken a paperclip from his jacket pocket and was twisting it round and round in his fingers.

'Well, I was planning to leave at seven or eight,' he smiled, 'but I went to see her and say goodbye.' He paused. 'And you know how it is.'

The young man was grinning again. He pursed his lips and nodded. He pulled a half-bottle of whiskey from his pocket, and began to sip from it.

'Yes,' said Ray Priest, 'yes, I know how it is.'

The young man offered his bottle, but Ray Priest shook his head and said, 'No thanks.' Sheet lightning lit up the whole sky.

'I thought I might get a waiter's job,' said the young man, 'there's plenty of those down around Kerry. It's the tourists.'

'Yes,' said Ray Priest, 'that's easy work to find.'

'Not for me it isn't,' said the young man, quietly.

'Oh yeah,' said Ray Priest, 'why's that?'

The young man stared out through the windscreen. He wiped away the condensation with the back of his hand.

'I'm not good with work,' he said, 'this'll be the first real job I ever had.'

'Yes,' laughed Ray Priest, 'I have a son like that. Spent four years in college, now he doesn't seem to know what to do.' The young man laughed.

'I wasn't in college,' he said, 'I was in jail.'

Ray Priest swerved around a dark corner.

'Oh yeah,' he said, as casually as possible, 'what were you in jail for?'

'For killing somebody,' the young man said, in a matter-of-fact voice, and he looked at Ray Priest, and he smiled. His teeth were yellow. 'For hammering somebody's brains in,' he said, 'with a spade.' He threw back his head and slugged from his bottle of whiskey.

'Jesus,' said Ray Priest.

'Yup,' said the young man, 'I came in one night to find this guy with my girlfriend, so it was wham, bam, thank you mam.' He smiled again. 'With the spade, I mean,' he explained, 'not with my girlfriend.' Then the young man laughed, in a high-pitched way, like the whinny of a horse.

'Well,' said Ray Priest, uncertainly, 'how come they let you out?'

'Oh, I escaped,' said the young man. 'What I did, I dug this tunnel, you see, and I escaped, and went down to South America for a while. Then I came back here, and nobody recognised me.'

'Nobody recognised you?' said Ray Priest.

'Yeah,' said the young man, 'with the face change.' The young man began to laugh. He snorted with laughter, then he leaned over and slapped Ray Priest on the thigh. 'April Fool, man,' he cackled, 'it's after midnight, it's April Fool's Day.'

Ray Priest glanced at his watch. The young man was right. It was April the first. He sighed with relief.

'Fuck it,' laughed Ray Priest, 'you had me worried then.'

'Heh heh heh,' laughed the young man.

'I mean,' giggled Ray Priest, 'I thought, Christ, here I am stuck in a car with a guy I don't know who's a fucking murderer.'

'Heh heh heh,' laughed the young man, and he wiped his eyes.

'So you weren't really in jail then?' said Ray Priest. 'I mean, you didn't really kill somebody.'

'Oh, come on, Ray,' smiled the young man, 'I mean, what do you think?' The gearbox made a churning sound.

The young man slowly held his hands up in front of his face. He stared at them, as though he had never seen his own hands before. He flexed his fingers, making his hands into fists, then into claws, staring at them all the time.

'Do these look like a killer's hands,' he smiled, 'to you, I mean?'

'I don't know,' stammered Ray, 'I wouldn't know about that.'

'Take it from me, Ray,' the young man grinned, 'they don't.'

'How do you know my name,' said Ray Priest, 'just as a matter of interest?'

'Oh, just a guess,' the young man said, his face cracking into a grin. He tapped the side of his nose, and winked. Then he laughed out loud, and he said, 'No, I'm just kidding you, Ray, I saw it written there, on your suitcase, in the back.'

Ray Priest smiled, but he felt a little uneasy. They were moving through dark and tiny roads now, with no light, and high hedges on either side. They drove on through the lashing rain for some time, and the young man kept laughing, 'Heh heh heh', and staring at his hands. Ray Priest didn't want to admit it, but he was scared, and he knew that he was lost too. He stopped his car, flicked on the light and began to read the map, glancing from the corner of his eye at the young man.

He was drumming on the dashboard again. He held the whiskey bottle to his lips and blew across the rim. It made a lonely sound.

'Do you fight with your wife, Ray?' he said.

'I'm sorry?' said Ray Priest.

'Your old lady, Ray,' he said, 'do you fight with her?'

'Sometimes,' said Ray Priest, after a moment. 'I mean, we're married.'

'What do you fight about, Ray? Tell me.'

'I told you, we're married, we fight about the usual things.'

'That's a terrible thing, Ray,' said the young man, and he shook his head ruefully. 'A gulf between a man and a woman is a terrible thing.' The young man's fingers tapped on the bottle.

'Look, I'm trying to read the map here,' said Ray Priest.

A thick mist was coming down now. When the car began to move again, Ray felt the tyres splash through mud, and he heard long branches hammer on the roof. The car turned a corner. And then very suddenly the yellow mist was so thick that Ray could not see the road in front of his eyes. He slowed down quickly into first, and inched carefully along the track.

'We're lost, Ray,' said the young man, 'we could be anywhere.'

'Yes. Maybe we should go back,' Ray laughed, 'I really don't know about this.'

'Don't be afraid, Ray,' the young man whispered, and he reached over and touched the back of Ray Priest's hand. 'I'm here.'

Suddenly there was a loud crash, and a sound of breaking glass. The car shuddered and stopped. Ray Priest heard a low screaming sound, and something heavy falling over out on the road.

'Christ,' said Ray Priest.

Ray Priest and the young man sat very still for a moment. When they got out of the car, they were in a tiny bog track, with thick trees and undergrowth on both sides. The young man pulled a torch from his pocket. The rain roared. In a few seconds Ray Priest was soaked to the skin. And the air was thick with fog, so that he could barely even make out the young man's body. The young man faced the road, in front of the car. He stood very still, with his hands on the back of his head. Even with the fog lights full on, they could see nothing, except the thick, yellow fog, swirling. The young man did not look afraid.

'Who's there?' shouted the young man. 'Who's out there?' But there was no reply.

'We were only doing ten,' said Ray Priest, 'we couldn't have hurt anyone, could we?'

The young man began to walk away. He walked forward, into the fog. Then he seemed to be gone and Ray Priest was alone. All he could hear was the sound of the rain, pouring into the hedges, hissing all around him.

'Stay with me,' he shouted to the young man, but there was no answer. Ray Priest laughed, 'I mean, Jesus, don't leave me here.'

'I'm here, Ray,' came a horrible voice behind him, 'you don't get rid of me that easy.'

Ray Priest turned around quickly, and the young man was standing behind the car now.

'Quit fooling around,' said Ray Priest, 'this isn't a game.'

'April Fool's Day, Ray,' laughed the young man, and he shone his torch up onto his face, and leered. 'Heh heh heh,' he sniggered, 'that's poetry, isn't it? April Fool's Day, Ray. I'm a poet and I know it.' The young man walked to the front of the car again. He bent down low. He squatted, in the mud, and he held his hands over his eyes. Ray Priest stood beside him. He tried to look straight down the road, but he could see nothing in the mist. 'I don't know what we hit, Ray,' the young man sighed. 'Now, that's very annoying.'

Thunder roared. Rain came surging down into the backroad, beating against the leaves, so hard that it made a sound like applause.

Then suddenly the fog was full of strange sounds, the sound of men shouting, and animal noises too, on all sides, wild and hysterical. Ray Priest felt the hair on the back of his neck stand up. He was cold and frightened.

'What's going on?' he laughed.

'Shhh,' hissed the young man, suddenly, and he put a finger in front of his mouth, listening. He stared straight at Ray Priest, with wide eyes. And after a moment, he smiled. 'Cows, Ray.' I know that sound. Must be the lightning. That's the sound of cows, going crazy.'

Ray and the young man stood still on the road, trying to gauge from where the sound was coming. In front of the car they could still see nothing. Then, behind them, the wind lifted and the mist began to clear.

They walked back down the road a little, and the rain was falling so hard that they could not hear their footsteps on the road. Rain poured down the back of Ray Priest's shirt. His damp jeans clung to his thighs. He looked over the hedge at one side of the road, and the young man looked over the other.

'Cows, Ray,' shouted the young man. 'Come over here. I knew it.'

Lightning flashed through the sky, huge forks of lightning.

Black and brown cows were dashing up and down the field, with no direction, crashing into haystacks and trees, stumbling to their knees in the mud. Thin men in black oilskin coats were running through the field too, waving their arms, trying to stop the cows from escaping. The beams of their flashlights moved through the darkness, like the beams of many lighthouses, all gone mad. Rain was lashing down now. The men ran around the field, falling over each other in the dark.

'Look at that, Ray,' shouted the young man, and he pointed his shaking hand. Up on the hill behind the field, the little barn was on fire. Great plumes of dark blue smoke rose into the sky. Inside the barn was glowing red and purple. Behind the barn was a house, and all the lights were on in the windows. Everywhere men and women seemed to be running, shouting. A thunderclap boomed across the fields. 'Isn't that something?' Wind screamed through the trees. Rushing water gurgled in the ditches.

'Let's get out of here,' said Ray Priest, 'I don't like this one bit.'

The young man and Ray walked back to the front of the car. Now the mist had drifted a little from there too. The road was dark, but in the fog lights, something was moving. Ray Priest and the young man walked forwards.

'Fuck,' said the young man.

'Oh my God,' said Ray Priest.

A fat white cow was lying on its back in the ditch, wrapped up in barbed wire, with its legs in the air. Its eyes were terrified. It made a whimpering sound, like a baby crying. When it saw Ray and the young man it took a sudden fright, and began to struggle. Barbed wire bit deeper into its flesh, at the udder, and it opened its jaws and howled.

'Oh, Jesus,' gasped Ray Priest, 'what'll we do?'

The young man seemed not to even notice that Ray Priest was there now. He stared at the cow. He took a step towards it.

'Cool it, lover,' he said. He ran his hand over his soaking leather jacket. Then he stretched out his fingers.

And then, with one sudden lunge, the cow flipped itself over onto its belly and clambered out of the ditch, ripping a gash in the side of its leg. It looked terrified. Thick blood stained its white coat. It staggered from side to side on the road, its heels sliding on the wet stones. It charged into the hedge, but could not get through. Its eyes were wild now. It bent its head low and ran at the hedge again. It hit its head on a fence post and staggered backwards, staring at the young man with fury in its eyes.

The young man stepped in front of the cow and he held up his arms.

'Whoo there,' he said, 'easy now, girl.' The cow reared up on its back legs, clawing at the air, like a wild horse. It opened its mouth and bellowed. The young man lunged forward and grabbed its ears. 'Whoo now,' he said, 'you're alright, babe,' and he slapped the cow gently on the haunches. The cow screamed again. The young man grabbed the cow's head and swung backwards, putting all of his weight on the cow, so that it could not move.

'Let's just get out of here,' stammered Ray Priest.

'We can't do that, Ray,' panted the young man, 'these cows are somebody's bread and butter.'

Ray Priest ran his hands through his soaking hair. He found himself wondering about what his wife was doing right at that moment. Rain spilled down his face. Again the thunder came crashing through the sky. Ray Priest turned and looked straight down the road. What he saw there made him wish that he was anywhere else.

A gang of cows came around the corner at the end of the track, snorting, moving along in a frightened mass, lowing mournfully. They were moving along quickly now, trotting, jostling one another, heads down low, splashing through the mud, and the sound they made was like the sound of some terrible engine. Ray Priest stood very still, listening to the cold and fearful sound. When he looked at the young man, he was staring back at him.

'Fuck,' shouted the young man, 'do something, Ray, will you?'

Ray Priest didn't even stop to think. He stepped into his car, breathing hard. He turned the key and roared. He jammed it into first, started to three-point-turn it. The front wheel clanged into the ditch, and when Ray Priest tried to move, he heard the wheel whirring round in the mud. He turned and stared over his shoulder. He was panting hard. Although he was cold, sweat pumped through his face. The young man was standing in the middle of the road now, in front of the cows, waving his arms again, jumping up and down. The cows were screaming, charging at him. Steam came streaming from their nostrils. They bellowed and roared. As they got closer, the young man went down on his knees. Ray Priest glanced at his steering wheel. He hit his horn, hard.

The sound of the horn blared through the backroad. The cows stopped, began staring up at the sky, looking confused. One or two kept running. They passed the young man, knocked him over sideways into the ditch and loped along, snorting. But Ray Priest's car was blocking the track now, and there was no escape for them. They stared at Ray Priest, sniffing at his car.

Then men in black seemed to come tumbling over the ditches, forcing their way through the hedges, brandishing flashlights and sticks, their breathless faces and their clothes cut to shreds. They ran up and down, hauling at the cows, tying ropes around their necks, bellowing orders at each other. Ray saw one of them help to drag the young man out of the ditch and lift him to his feet. Cows' faces leered in at him through the window of his car, stupid, curious, blank. Their faces bumped against the windows. Their long pink tongues licked at the glass.

'Fuck off,' shouted Ray Priest, 'get out of here.' He lifted his hands to his wet face and found, to his surprise, that he wanted to cry.

Then, through his fingers, he saw an older man come weaving through the bewildered cows towards his car.

'Who are you?' shouted the dark-faced, unshaven man, shining his flashlight into Ray Priest's eyes. He had a double-barrel shotgun slung over his back, and underneath his oilskin he was wearing pyjamas. When he leaned forward, rain spilled from the brim of his hat. Ray Priest rolled down his window.

'I'm Ray Priest,' he stammered, 'I'm nobody. What happened here?'

The farmer said that lightning had struck his barn, and the cows had gone wild. He was very grateful indeed to Ray, he said, for acting so quickly, moving his car like that, to block off the road. If they'd made it as far as the dual carriageway, he said, his cows would have just run amok and killed somebody.

Ray Priest sighed. He said that it was the least he could do.

The farmer said the fire was out now. It was just a flash fire, something you saw in the country when the weather was strange as it had been lately. No real harm was done, he said, everything had blown over now.

'And who's that?' the farmer said then, nodding at the young man.

'Oh, that's just a friend of mine,' said Ray. The young man came over to the car. His face was grazed, and he was holding his left wrist, but he was still smiling. He nodded at Ray and the farmer, then he put his hand across his forehead and he stared up at the smoking barn, with a weird kind of amazement in his eyes.

The farmer pinched his nose and began to laugh, guiltily.

'You know, when we saw you down here on the road, we thought you might have been those two prisoners,' said the farmer, 'those two that broke out of Portlaoise tonight. The IRA boy, and the rapist.'

The young man turned around very slowly. He stared hard at the farmer. He began to laugh. He threw back his head and laughed hard, 'Heh heh heh', and he clapped the farmer on the back.

'Now that's a good one,' laughed the young man, 'you and me, Ray, desperadoes, isn't that something?' He looked in the window of Ray Priest's car, licking the rain from his lips, and he smiled.

The farmer laughed too, a little nervously. Ray Priest shivered. He felt his heart stop, and then start beating again.

'We don't know anything about prisoners, do we, Ray?' smiled the young man.

'No,' said Ray Priest, quietly, and he swallowed hard.

The farmer looked a little embarrassed. His men were pointing at him, from under the trees, and giggling together.

'Well,' the farmer muttered, 'it's late. I suppose you want to be getting back to Dublin now.'

'Yes,' said the young man, 'us hardened criminals have crimes to do, don't we, Ray?' He punched the farmer playfully on the shoulder, then he grabbed the farmer's hand and shook it hard.

'I thought you were going to Cork,' said Ray Priest.

'I never said that, Ray,' said the young man, looking surprised, 'I said I was going wherever you were going.'

'Well, I'm going home,' said Ray Priest, 'I've changed my mind.' The young man shrugged, and he smiled again, and he looked around at the wet fields.

'Well, that's me stuck, isn't it?' he said.

'Maybe we could give you a bed here?' said the farmer, and the young man stared at him, very intensely.

'Well,' said the young man, 'that would be very kind.'

'Sure you won't stay too?' the farmer said to Ray, putting his hand on the handle of the car door. 'You'd be more than welcome.'

'No, no,' said Ray, 'I have to get home.'

'Yes,' smiled the young man, 'Ray has a family, don't you, Ray? We wouldn't want anything to happen to Ray's family, would we, Ray?'

'Where am I?' said Ray Priest. 'I'll need some directions.'

'Well,' said the farmer's son, 'you need to go back the way you came, into Abbeyleix, straight through the other side, and you're on the road for Dublin.'

'You're going to be taking the long way home,' the farmer laughed, 'I'll warn you that much. Come on now, do stay with us.'

'No, no. That's OK,' snapped Ray Priest, 'I'm in a rush.' The farmer looked sad.

'Oh well,' he said, 'if you insist.'

'He insists, he insists,' smiled the young man, 'Ray has his responsibilities to think of, don't you, Ray?'

'Yes,' said Ray Priest, 'yes, I do.'

Ray Priest sat in his car for a while, watching the farmer and his helpers and the young man, as they walked up through the fields and back towards the house. The rain had stopped now, and had given way to the lightest of drizzle. But the wind was still whistling hard and cold, down from the mountain and in across the bog.

He drove back slowly into Abbeyleix, then up through Arderin and Mountmellick. He ground his foot into the accelerator and began to drive faster then, small towns flashing past the window of his car, Kilcomer, Rathangan, Naas, until the orange haze of Dublin was within his reach again.

When he walked into the bedroom, his wife sat up suddenly. She leaned on her elbows and gaped at him. Her eyes were wide. She looked a little frightened.

'Ray Priest,' she said, 'where were you?'

'Don't start now, Maria,' he said to his wife, 'I'm warning you.' His wife looked like she was about to cry. She said nothing. Ray Priest sat on the edge of the bed, with his head in his hands, staring into the mirror. He felt bad for speaking to his wife like that. 'I just went for a drive, I needed to think.'

'It's five-thirty,' she said, 'what were you thinking about?'

'I fell asleep,' Ray Priest said. 'I was sitting up on Killiney Hill, watching the lightning. I was thinking about you and me.'

'Your clothes,' she said, 'you're covered in mud, Ray.'

'I fell over,' he said, 'I tripped outside and I fell.' His wife smiled.

'You're such a dreamer, Ray Priest,' she laughed, 'but I don't suppose I'd want you to change.'

His wife lay back in the bed. She watched while Ray Priest opened his shirt, screwed it up and threw it on the chair. She watched while he pulled off his boots, his socks, unzipped his muddy jeans, peeled them down over his wet thighs. When he crawled into bed, shivering, she turned away from him, and he lay close to her, with his chest against her back. She flicked out the light. For some minutes, they lay very still, without speaking. Ray Priest felt the warmth of his wife's body spreading through his limbs. His feet smelt bad. His throat felt sore. When in the end he spoke, his voice was hoarse.

'Did you hear the news?' he said.

'Yes,' she answered sleepily, 'things are bad in Liberia.'

'Did you hear anything about prisoners?' he said. 'Escaped prisoners, something like that.'

'Mmmm,' she said, 'they caught them an hour after they got out, in some pub in Portlaoise.'

The shadow of the rain on the window danced up and down the bedroom walls.

'You sure?' he said.

''Course I am,' she sighed, 'all safely tucked away.'

His wife yawned a laugh. 'I thought you'd left me, Ray Priest,' she said. 'I thought you were never coming back.'

She moved her feet against his, took his arm, wrapped it around her body, placed his hand on her stomach. Ray Priest's face felt hot.

'You know I'd never do that,' he said, softly, 'I just got lost for a little while.'

'You're a fool,' she teased him, 'an old April fool.' and then suddenly she was asleep again. The last rolls of thunder rumbled over the faraway mountains.

Ray Priest leaned over his wife's body and he pushed her hair away from her sleeping face. He gazed at her, with love in his heart, and then, very gently, he kissed his wife on the side of her mouth.

'I'll always love you, Maria,' he said.

'Mmmm,' she sighed, in her sleep.

Ray Priest clung to his wife's body. As he drifted into sleep, he began to see things clearly. He thought about his night, about the loneliness of a man who finds that he has to run from love. And he knew in those moments that love is not always about freedom. He could see it then, with the clarity that only half-sleep brings. He could see that love is often just a homecoming, and little more. And that the journey home of the heart is sometimes the longest of all.

The Bedouin Feast

TUNISIA. The way my friend Joseph stood in the aisle of the coach. The start of that sweltering night. I can see it still, that wild look in his eye as he staggered past me, hands outstretched, rocking like a schizophrenic tightrope walker, with the bus ploughing fury through the dustclouds.

This, and the breathtaking, crazy heat are the things I remember. Weird. Two vague things, you would think, but they're clear and sharp in my mind. The way some dreams are when you think back. Heat hammering from the sky. Seeping out of my skin. The taste of that night. Oranges and sunshine and the stench of duty-free perfume in the front of the coach. So hot that the snakes lay in the street with their tongues hanging out and the driver kept swerving to squash them.

'Hey, Tony,' Joseph screamed, grabbing the headrest, 'c'mere a minute, you bleedin' fairy.'

I looked at Marie. I asked her what he was doing. She sighed and wiped her forehead. Then she did her angel's smile. She told me that Joseph was asking Tony for permission to tell a few jokes. This was the usual thing apparently, when Joseph was drunk. Started thinking he was Irish Catholicism's answer to Lenny Bruce.

She's a witty girl, Marie. She really is. For an English girl, I mean.

In work, he never behaved like that. No. There he was almost polite. Quiet-cigarette-in-the-toilets type. But holidays, you see. They bring out the worst in people. Holidays and drink. In the office he had hardly any friends at all, to tell the truth, except for me, and even that was often touch-and-go. I mean, *we* were only friends because of the night I'd dragged him home after the Christmas bash. I must have been feeling charitable. Fellow Irishman, all of that. I must have been drunk, too. That night I met her, when she opened the door glowing in lace and saw him puking like a fruit machine over the dahlias, with me trying to shake her hand and explain. 'I believe this is your better half,' I said. The way she bent down, low over the eiderdown, when we were putting him to bed.

That was when The Bitch was still around of course. We talked about her, me and Marie, that night while Joseph lay snoring inside. I don't know how we got onto it. She made delicious coffee and we ended up talking about my marriage, until four in the morning. God knows how.

Jesus, it's not as if I don't like him. I'm not saying that. I mean the guy's a friend of mine.

*

Tony was the tour guide. He had an obsession with Elvis Presley. That was about the only good thing you could say about him. On the coach, he kept looking over his shoulder and beaming hysterically at us, like he wanted us to get Joseph to sit down.

'No way, Tone,' I thought, 'you get paid good money to deal with shit like this.'

I sat back hard and closed my eyes. My lips tasted of salt. The coach shuddered around a corner. Somebody groaned. I think it was me.

I couldn't sleep. And when I opened my eyes again Marie's face looked worried, and wet with sweat. So I did something weird. I tried to hold her hand. I don't know why. I grabbed her fingers between my two hands and kind of patted her, as if she were some kind of furry animal as it turned out, not that this was the intention. It just happened that way. I always get these things wrong.

She laughed then, as though I had done something

ridiculous. She looked away. She pressed her nose against the glass. But I couldn't really criticise her. Not in these circumstances.

I mean it was her idea to bring me on holiday, after all, not Joseph's. She thought it would help, after The Bitch fucked off with that musclebound neanderthal of hers, took the best years of my life, left nothing except the fucking phone bill and the shrivelled remains of my ego. She called me up when I was half-way through a bottle of whiskey. Marie I mean. Not The Bitch. That would have been too much.

She said, 'Look, Sweetie, don't get upset, come to Tunisia with us.'

Joseph had told her all about it. I could have cried. Well, I did cry, but that was different. See, that's the kind of girl she is. The kind that wants to help. She tells me what a brick I am. Never done telling me. How she sees me like the big brother she never had. How she can really *trust* me with her secrets. And their sex life. Jesus. I'm a cross between John Boy Walton and Doctor Ruth. *I* know more about her than Joseph does. Sometimes I wish I'd never met her. Him too. Especially now.

'You're a very feminine man,' she tells me. 'I just feel so incredibly safe with you, because I know you're not going to try a move on me.' I think she means that as a compliment. But if I hear it once more I'll scream. I really will. Christ, if only she knew.

'I just love Irish men,' she says, 'they're so untamed or something. So un-hung-up, compared to English men. That's why I like Joseph, I suppose.'

'We're not all like him,' I tell her.

'You are,' she says, 'don't be modest. Deep down, you are.'

Modest. Love it.

I mean, it's not that I wasn't grateful. Just that Joseph was drunk before he even got on the plane, turned up at the airport late, singing 'Wrap the Green Flag Round Me,

Boys', three sheets in the wind, insisted on searching the little black man beside him for semtex, groping inside his jacket. When he'd sobered up, he and Marie spent the rest of the flight pulling lovey-dovey faces and chewing the lips off each other at 30,000 feet. She calls him Bubble. Pass the sick bag. I don't know what she sees in him. I really don't. He tried to persuade her to have sex with him in the toilet of the plane. I'm serious. I heard him. I mean that's the level we're at here.

The hotel was tiny. It smelt of stale coffee and dirty sheets and the madwoman in the lobby kept trying to show me her underwear. And as soon as we arrived the waiter grinned and said, 'You three look knackered.' His face was dark brown. He was from Tunis but he spoke the few words of English he knew with a Peckham accent. Obviously, this was supposed to be impressive. But when I heard that I just bloody knew it was going to be one of those trips. My friend Joseph – naturally – thought it was hilarious. He slapped the waiter on the back and roared with laughter.

'Knackered,' he said, 'Jesus, that's exactly what we are, man. You fucking said it. C'mere pal, do you've any Irish blood in you?'

Nights, I could hear them in the next room. Her and him. I lay awake in that heat, listening, listening, dripping sweat, wishing something would happen. They'd do it for a few minutes, rest for a while, talk and laugh, do it again. And the only noise that interrupted them was the mosquitos buzzing and the wail of the holy man from the mosque down by the beach.

'*Allah o akbar,*' he sang, '*Allah o akbar,*' all night long.

The muezzin, apparently. That's what they're called out there, the salvation merchants. So it says in my book. Muezzin. Funny word. Sounds like some kind of obscure venereal disease. Christ. Now I'm beginning to sound like him. Strike that. Just forget I said that. OK? You see? That's the kind of person he is. Infectious.

Anyway, '*Allah o akbar*'s what they said. God is great. And boy, did they say it often. Middle of the night? No problem. Thundering out of the loudspeaker, drowning out the gymnastics next door. But to be fair, I must say, they really are very devout people, if a little public about it. It must shock them. It really must. The things that go on, I mean.

You see, it isn't that we aren't friends. How do I explain? It's just that when he's drinking, my friend Joseph is a different man. He tells awful jokes. He laughs at them himself and he slaps you hard on the thigh if you don't crease up. What he does, right – this'll give you an idea – he grabs the inside flesh of your thigh and squeezes hard, with his pointing finger and his thumb, laughing like a madman. That's the type we're talking about here. I mean, it hurts like shit but he thinks it's hilarious. He doesn't mean it, but when he's drinking he has a crazy streak. He can't be responsible for things. I think it's because of his mother. She did something to him, I'm certain of it. Marie keeps hinting in that general direction. 'Irish mothers,' she says, meaningfully. As though that excuses anything.

He embarrasses you on the beach, too, when all you want to do is lie there and he's chasing topless girls, trying to put ice cream cones down the back of their pants. Never a thought for Marie. She doesn't mind exactly. I suppose she's used to him. But I mean, if I had treated The Bitch like that she would have fucked off and left me. Well, she did fuck off and leave me, of course. I suppose what I mean is, she would have fucked off and left me sooner. But that, as the lift operator said, is another story. The Bitch.

The Bedouin Feast was Joseph's idea. Fun, he said. It sounded like fun. Normally I'm not one for these excursions, but I was bored sick with everything else and, anyway, Marie pleaded with me. She said he'd be impossible to manage if I didn't tag along.

'No way,' I told her. 'I'm not his nursemaid.'

'You know that's not what I think,' she sighed. 'That's not why I invited you.'

'Do I?' I said. 'Oh do I? Really?'

Her long hair sort of fell around her face. The eyes looked up at me then, bright, two little animals in a cave.

'Of course you do,' she smiled. 'We're friends.'

'Then you shouldn't force me into some phoney tourist beanfeast,' I huffed, 'I can't stand those things.'

'That's alright,' she said, 'I mean, there's no pressure.'

'Fine,' I said.

'That's arranged, then,' she said, 'Joseph and me'll go by ourselves.'

'Fine, fine, fine,' I said. 'Fine.'

'Hunky dory,' she said, *'pas de problème.'*

My God, she's beautiful when she's trying to tell you lies.

*

That night, on the bus, steaming away in my shorts, the heat made the backs of my thighs stick to the leatherette. My forehead stung with sunburn. The back of my neck felt raw, like someone had peeled off a layer of my skin. My stomach felt sick, too. I really wasn't in great shape. Animals in the water apparently. Little microbes or something. Leapfrogging through your guts.

I stared at Joseph, the way his hand was leaning on the driver's shoulder, the way he was swaying from side to side, swigging from his beer. So bloody confident. Cocky as anything. I couldn't make up my mind whether what I was feeling was embarrassment or envy. Maybe a bit of both. I just don't know. I didn't like it anyway.

Careering out of Hammamet, I found myself wondering about what The Bitch was doing right then, and about one night when we'd made love in the grass down by the beach in Killiney and got sand in our parts. God she was gorgeous too. So together. So capable. Like Marie in a way. Not as soft, perhaps. Well, not really like her at all, in fact, come to think of it. I'm always doing that. Comparing. Everyone tells me I have to stop.

Joseph threw the microphone from hand to hand, like Tom Jones in bermuda shorts, spitting into it to see if it worked.

'Testing, testing,' he simpered. He reached down to the tape deck and turned Elvis off. 'My wife, my wife,' he cawed, 'I won't say she's ugly but her face would turn milk sour.'

Jesus.

A few people laughed. But it only encouraged him. So he made another 'joke', which I'm just not prepared to repeat, frankly. All I will say is that it involved a bishop, a well-endowed donkey and a policeman's helmet. Then he offered to take down his trousers.

'Oh Christ,' sighed Marie, 'he's pissed again.'

Tony flicked Elvis back on. Then he grabbed the microphone and said the jokes were a bit blue really, for this time of the night.

'I know we're all on holidays, Joseph,' he chuckled nervously, 'but we don't want the old standards to go completely out the window. I mean, after all, we're representing something here.'

'Turn that crap off,' somebody shouted.

'*Uh, baby lemme be*,' crooned Tony, '*you lervin' teddy bayuh.*'

When we stopped for what Tony called 'little boys time', Joseph pissed high against the side of the bus and the Arab kids laughed at him. I looked down at him through the window. He wiggled his ungainly member, sending spurts of orange urine up the window at my face. The Arab kids screamed with laughter. I could feel my cheeks going red. Tunes, Tony called them. The Tunisians. Loony Tunes.

'Went to a pub on the moon once,' sniggered Joseph, clambering back in. 'Didn't like it. No atmosphere.'

'Get off,' somebody shouted. The bus driver made the

engine roar. He looked angry. He said something pretty brisk to Tony. Tony made Joseph sit down beside him.

'So this guy goes to the doctor, you see, with an awful pain in . . .'

Tony grabbed the microphone.

'Right, then, campers,' he interrupted, 'we're just going to pick up at the Desert Song Apartments, and then we'll be off to the Bedouin Feast. And we're a full coach tonight, so please, feet off the seats and no lying down. There'll be plenty of that later on, eh?' He did his irritating laugh then. 'Once you get a few bottles of the local brew down you, I mean, you cheekies. And by the way, there's a twenty-dinar fine for anyone who redecorates the upholstery.' A chorus of puking noises wafted through the bus. '*Charmant*,' Tony said, rummaging for his notes.

'What have acid rain and monkeys got in common?' giggled Joseph. 'They both fuck up trees.'

Tony grabbed the microphone again. He coughed.

'The Bedouin Feast is an ancient Arab celebration,' he informed us.

'The ancient . . . er . . . Arabs used to gather in the oases at night, in a big tent, with plenty of grub and plenty of ale, have a good old knees-up, loads of fun. It's all very authentic, where we're going.' A stunningly unimpressed silence filled the bus. Tony looked at his notes again. 'The tent has been constructed,' he quoted, pleadingly, 'with reference to medieval design.'

'Ooooooooooo,' chirped the white-sox brigade, down the back.

'My mother-in-law,' screamed Joseph, 'I won't say she's ugly, but . . .'

'Sit down, you,' chuckled Tony, 'or I'll be very miffed.'

Joseph pushed past me and went down the back of the bus, to where the white soxers were. He'd been hanging around with them all week, actually. Keith and Keith and Baz and Keith. He just wasn't interested in seeing the sights.

He left myself and Marie to it while he got wrecked every night in the hotel disco and slept it off next day on the beach.

That was a mistake.

⋆

I cried outside the golden mosque and she took my face in her hands.

'I just want it to stop,' I said. Her body felt warm and sweaty through the cotton. She smelt of suntan oil and peppermints. Her lips looked soft.

'Oh, we're such good friends,' she smiled, 'let me give you a big, sisterly hug. Here. I just can't bear to see you like this.'

⋆

Way in the distance, the sun glinted over a field of white crosses.

'OK,' Tony said, nervously consulting the notes again, 'a bit of Tune history on the way. The local war cemetery contains the graves of the many thousands of British soldiers who gave their lives in the desert campaign of World War Two. If you look to your left now, as we pass . . .'

'Fuck off,' came the chant, from the back, led of course by You Know Who, 'fuck off, fuck off'. They were singing it to the tune of 'Amazing Grace', cackling like bloody schoolboys.

'Suit yourself,' Tony pouted, 'you unpatriotic beasts,' and he put on 'The King: Live from Caesar's Palace' for the fifth time. Very loud. He started singing along again. Defiantly.

You ainna nuthin burra houn dawg
Cryin awl a time.

Marie put her head in her hands. I patted her thigh, reassuringly I thought. But she did one of her strange looks, and I went back to doing the crossword.

'You're not . . .' she said, and then she stopped.

'No,' I said, 'I'm not,' despite the fact that I hadn't a clue what she was talking about.

'Nearly there, campers,' called Tony, 'altogether now.'

You ainna niver cawra rabbi
And you ainna no frind amine.

I had the vaguest of feelings that something was going to go wrong.

*

Beside the cluster of coaches we all got given a little blue ticket. Blue was for the English-speaking tent. There were four tents in all, arranged in a sort of four-leaf clover shape. One tent for each language. The acts took turns in different tents, Tony explained. That way everybody got to see everything. Yellow was for German. Brown was for French. Pink was for Portuguese. European Unity in action.

'There's no flies on these people,' said Tony, 'believe you me.'

Efficient-looking Belgians snapped each other in front of the barking camels. Bearded Germans queued up at a painted board behind which you could stand, stick your head through a hole, and get your photo taken looking like the sphinx. Bleary-eyed, insect-swatting English swarmed through the souvenir stalls, waving plastic sabres and 'I heart Tunisia' boxer shorts. The coach drivers, all dressed in black, sat in a circle in the middle of the car park, spitting on the ground, listening to a soccer match on a transistor radio, passing around a pipe. We queued and took photographs of an old woman who was baking bread in a big oven.

Apparently called Fatima. Or so it said in seven languages on the placard round her neck.

'Look at her,' simpered Tony, 'there's nothing she likes more than getting her photo took, is there, chuck?' He tickled the fat Arab woman under the chin. She smiled and held out her hand for a coin.

We waited for Joseph to get off the bewildered-looking camel and join the queue. His eyes were pale and fragile and watery. He looked a little unsteady on his feet. I knew he'd been smoking the local product again. Of course, he denied it. But I could tell. He had a way of being able to sniff it out. Any kind of trouble. Some kind of bloody radar for it.

The 'tent' was made of concrete and see-through plastic. In the middle was a large circle of sand and sawdust, lit up by disco lights and electric arrangements made up to look like flaming torches. Around this was a banked-up ring of tables and seats, for maybe three hundred punters. In the middle of the circle, a fat woman in a tinfoil bikini was belly dancing to 'I Should Be so Lucky' by Kylie Minogue. There was a vague smell of horseshit and aftersun. Marie said it looked very authentic, and I wondered how she'd know. She said something about Lawrence of Arabia.

'Did you ever see eyes,' she sighed, 'like Peter O'Toole's?' I felt jealous. I have to admit it.

A thick-necked, sulky guy in a kaftan showed us to our table. I gave him a tip, which he stared at, well-rehearsed disbelief in his eyes, the bloody nerve.

Way across the ring I could see Tony throwing his arms around a young woman tour guide, holding her by the wrists, whispering something in her ear. She threw back her blonde hair and laughed loud, slapping him in the chest as she walked away.

The heat was just getting ridiculous. I couldn't even *see* properly it was so hot now, reflecting off the plastic roof, blinding heat that had reduced everybody's clothes to wet rags. Her shirt clung to her chest. She wasn't wearing anything underneath. I tried to keep my eyes off.

Marie and Joseph and I sat down, and immediately the two old couples at the table stopped talking. They began peering intensely into their cups or up at the sky. My friend Joseph belched, farted, and lit a cigarette that smelt very funny.

One of the old men stared at him then. He had a round face, red peeling skin, an almost bald head. He didn't like Joseph one little bit. You could tell.

'You English, or what?' he said.

He wasn't completely bald, but the very top of his head was bald and sunburnt, and he'd let the hair on one side grow long and then combed it across his scalp. I hate people who do that. I think it's pathetic.

'I am,' explained Marie, 'but these two are Irish.'

'Oh,' he said, 'Irish.'

He didn't look happy. His wife touched his arm. He looked away.

'Please, Eric,' she whispered. 'We're on our holidays.'

She beamed at us, wiping her forehead with a tissue.

'I'm not saying anything,' he snapped, 'did I say anything?'

'No,' she said, 'you didn't.'

'No,' he said, 'I didn't. That's bloody right.'

'Dublin,' said Marie. 'Glass of water, please?' She's so capable in situations like this. You should see her. Nothing fazes her. It's living with him does it, I suppose.

'British, anyway,' said the other old man, 'I mean, we're all the same, really.' He passed the water jug, and a bottle of wine. 'Please have some?' he smiled. He looked nicer than the other man, though his wife looked depressed. She sat very still, just fanning the air with a copy of *The Mail on Sunday* magazine, licking at the sweat around her mouth.

'Dublin's fair city,' grinned the nice old man, 'Molly Malone, eh?'

Joseph looked like he was going to start something. I could see it.

He picked up the bottle, wiped the neck with his sleeve, and took a slug from it. Then he spat the purple liquid down the front of his T-shirt.

'Camelpiss,' he shuddered. The nice old man laughed, a little too loud.

'Yes, it does take a bit of getting used to,' he blushed. 'Anyway, Dublin *is* part of Britain, isn't it? It's like Scotland. Or Gibraltar.'

Marie started to explain that the Republic was actually a separate country. The nice old man seemed to have trouble with this. He wanted to know how come all the players on the Irish soccer team were English. Marie was interrupted by a raucous fanfare of horns that came screaming out of the speaker stack. I grabbed my friend Joseph by the wrist and told him to calm down. I could smell beer from his breath, and the faint odour of vomit.

'Chill out, man,' he gurgled, 'I'm on top of the situation.'

The way he talks. My God, who does he think he is?

Suddenly the lights went out, and spotlights picked out white circles in the ring. Excited murmurs ran around the crowd. People started cheering. The bald old man glared at me. I smiled. Then he turned away. I heard him say one word under his breath. Just one word. But very clear. You couldn't mistake it.

Murderers.

The troop of waiters marched out from behind the curtain, blowing kisses and pretending to fight, banging big metal plates with wooden spoons, in time to the music. They all wore red baggy trousers, black waistcoats. They marched round the ring a few times, waving, blowing more kisses, preening, conducting the audience as they clapped along with the music. One or two did cartwheels, the rest leapfrogged over each other. All very jolly. Then one waiter stopped in front of each section of the crowd, prancing from side to side, marching on the spot until the music, with an explosion of cymbals, suddenly stopped.

'BRITISH?' yelled our waiter.

'YEAH!' roared the crowd.

The waiter put his hands on his hips and a camp expression on his face. Then he stood on tiptoe, held one hand to his ear, closed his eyes, and roared '*BRITISH*?' again.

'YEAH!' roared the crowd.

'FUCKING *NO!*' roared Joseph. Marie slapped his thigh. The waiter ignored him.

'AND WHAT DOES THE BRITISH LIKES TO DRINK?' the waiter screamed. Silence. He scratched his head, in a parody of stupidity. Nervous laughter rippled through the crowd. 'Well?' he yelled. '*WATER*?'

'NO,' came the answer.

'*LEMONADE*?'

'NO'.

I could hear Tony cackling somewhere. And I could see the old man staring at Joseph again. He really didn't like him at all. He kept looking at him sidelong, with a little half-sneering grin on his face.

'*LAGER*?' screamed the waiter.

'YEAHHHHH!' roared the crowd.

'That's the ticket,' screeched the waiter.

Marie laughed, and I felt a little ashamed of her.

'*LOOOOOADSAMONEEEYYYYY!*' screeched the waiter.

'*LOOOOOADSAMONEEEYYYYY!*' screeched the crowd.

Prompted by their own waiter, the crowd opposite started yelling at us. They stood up and shook their fists. Their waiter stuck two fingers in the air. Then he turned away from us, and he bent over, slowly lowered his trousers, displaying his backside. His crowd squealed with laughter.

'OH YOU'RE ALL VERY QUIET OVER THERE, they sang,
OH YOU'RE ALL VERY QUIET OVER THERE

ALL VERY QUIET OH YOU'RE ALL VERY QUIET
OH YOU'RE ALL VERY QUIET OVER THERE.'

'Wankers,' hissed our waiter, 'fucking plonkers, innit?' He
grabbed his crotch and began jumping up and down,
shouting, 'Shut up your ugly mug' at the crowd opposite.
Around me, people started to wave their fists in the air.

'What a load of wallies,' they chanted.

'UGGY UGGY UGGY,' roared the waiter.

'OI OI OI,' roared the crowd.

Joseph sat with his head in his hands, rocking backwards
and forwards.

Marie's eyes were beautiful when she smiled. She looked
away from me, and out over the dark blue mountains.

In the distance we could hear the mournful call of the
muezzin, wafting down from the mosque on the hill.

'*Allah o akbar*,' he wailed. '*Allah o akbar*.' God is bloody
great. '*Allah, Allah, Allah*.'

Night was falling now. A man with a fez and a diseased-
looking monkey came and insisted on taking our photo. And
it must have been raining a little, although I don't remember
that. But you can see raindrops on the photo. Marie in the
middle of Joseph and me, with our arms around her. Little
blurs over our heads, like halos. Joseph leering, mouth open.

The waiter beamed and peeled off his waistcoat. He did a
Charles Atlas pose, and catcalls came from the seats beside
us. He put one hand on his hip, and the other to his forehead.

'Ooo, you are awful,' he pouted. Then he threw back his
head and laughed.

A flock of young women in gold bras and purple baggy
trousers appeared, distributing sweets, bits of melon, slivers
of orange, bottles of beer. You could see their nipples
through the cloth. I suppose it was the heat. Or maybe
it was deliberate. They weaved in and out of the tables,
handing out the icy bottles, making a great show of waggling
their chests in the old men's faces. When they had finished,

the waiter pulled a whistle from his pocket and blew it. He held up his hands, raised his eyebrows, pointed to his face.

'Ahmed,' he said, jabbing a finger at his face. 'Say hello Ahmed.'

'HELLO AHMED,' went the crowd. He looked pleased.

'Ladies and gentlemen,' he said, 'I now to sing for you traditional Arab song of welcome.'

'I was in Ireland once,' whispered the friendly old man, leaning over the table at me, 'years ago.'

'Shut your face, Geoffrey,' said his wife, 'he's singing.'

'We come here every year, you know, every year now since 1956. We were here in the war, you see.'

'How interesting,' smiled Marie.

'I think he's going to sing now,' I said.

The waiter held up his hand for quiet. He closed his eyes, very tightly, like he was waiting for some kind of inspiration to hit him. He clasped his hands in front of his chest like he was praying, and he began to rock, backwards and forwards on his heels.

Then he sang some words, which sounded vaguely familiar. He sang them in a soft nasal voice. And as his voice grew louder, he held his hands out towards us, palms facing the sky, gesturing with his fingers for us all to join in.

Chuckles of recognition rippled through the crowd. The nice old man turned to me.

'D'y' hear what he's singing?' he chuckled. 'The daft bugger.'

'Here we go, here we go, here we go,' chanted Ahmed.

'ERE WE GO, ERE WE GO, ERE WE GO, OH,' answered the crowd.

'Here we go, here we go, here we go,' chanted Ahmed.

'ERE WE GO, OH, ERE WE GO,' chanted the crowd, all except my friend Joseph. And me of course.

The waitresses shimmied off behind the curtain. Ahmed threw his tray to the ground, and scurried after one of them, making groping gestures at her ass. She whipped around, saw him, put her hands on her hips, pretended to look shocked. Ahmed put on an innocent face, marched back over to us. The crowd thought this was just hysterical.

'Get your tits out,' he sang,
Get your tits out,
Get your tits out for the lads.'

The two old men at our table laughed aloud.

Across from us, the crowd was in full spate now. They were dancing on the tables, clapping their hands in the air. Their waiter stood on a chair, waving two beer bottles above his head.

'ENGER-LAND, ENGER-LAND, ENGER-LAND,' they cheered. 'ONE GAZZA GASCOIGNE, THERE'S ONLY ONE GAZZA GASCOIGNE.'

Ahmed turned to us, not to be outdone.

'Altogether now,' he yelled, conducting with a cucumber as he sang.

'ARGEN-TINA, ARGEN-TINA
WOT'S IT LIKE TO LOSE A WAR?
WOT'S IT LIKE
TO LOSE A WAR?'

'OH, YOU'RE ALL BLOODY QUIET OVER THERE,' bellowed the crowd opposite.

'PLONKERS CHA CHA CHA, PLONKERS CHA CHA CHA,' Ahmed replied.

'Good Christ,' said Joseph, and he put his head in his hands.

'What's wrong, Bubble?' said Marie.

'Why is it,' he sighed, 'you put a few hundred English together, the first thing they do is split into two groups and start chanting at each other?'

'At least we don't shoot each other,' said the bald old man, quietly.

A large, thin black man in tight trousers swayed onto the centre podium, juggling earthenware jars.

'Look at him,' said my friend Joseph, loudly, 'bent as a Kerry road.'

The tall black man took a chair and balanced it on his chin. Then he called a young girl from the crowd and made her sit on the chair. Then he lifted the whole lot, with the girl sitting in it, up in the air and balanced it all on his forehead.

Marie and I applauded politely. Joseph looked unimpressed. The thin black man bowed gracefully, waving to the crowd.

The bald old man wasn't looking at him. He poured a glass of wine and drained it in one go. He looked hot. He poured another. His wife whispered something in his ear and he shrugged her off. He opened the top button of his shirt and ran his finger around the inside of the collar.

'You have to say that's brilliant,' said the nice old man. 'Really.'

Ahmed flashed us a smile, then he turned to face the opposite bit of the crowd again. Stamping his foot, he began to sing. Loud.

'You're a crowd of fucking Arabs over there,
 You're a crowd of fucking Arabs over there,
 You're a crowd of fucking Arabs,
 A crowd of fucking Arabs,
 A crowd of fucking Arabs over there.'

The two old men and the two old women chuckled, guiltily, as the song was picked up and bounced around the auditorium.

'A crowd of fucking Arabs,' laughed the nice old man, wiping his eyes, 'that's a good one.'

'At least they don't blooming blow each other up,' slurred the bald old man, 'not like some bleeding countries we could mention.'

'A CROWD OF FUCKING ARABS OVER THERE,' screamed the crowd.

'*I* say, at least they're not the fucking barbarians some people are. I'll give them that.'

His wife put one hand to her cheek.

'Eric, please,' she said, 'you know what you were told.'

'Shut up, you cow,' he snapped, and then he began to speak again.

'*Allah o akbar*,' sang the faraway voice.

'At least,' said the old man, very deliberately, 'they're not *complete* bloody savages.'

And that was when my friend Joseph stood up. He was red in the face. He was shaking. I thought he was going to hit somebody. He was drunk.

'Shut up, you,' he snarled at the old man. 'Just shut it, alright?'

'What's the matter with you, then?' said the old man, trying to sound brave, although now he looked afraid.

'You,' spat Joseph. 'You're the fucking matter.'

'Oh, I see,' said the old man, 'I see. Typical, innit?'

'What does "typical" mean?' growled Joseph.

The old man laughed, and took another mouthful of beer. He wiped his lips with the back of his hand. He laughed again.

'Well, I can't help it,' he said, 'if you're so stupid you can't understand the English language.'

'Now there's no call for that, mate,' said the nice old man.

'Who are you calling stupid?' said Joseph. 'You cunt.'

The old man didn't look afraid now. He looked angry. He stood up.

'Who are you talking to, Paddy?' he croaked.

Marie jumped up and grabbed my arm.

'Come on,' she said, 'let's find another table.'

'I'm talking to you, you miserable old fucker,' said Joseph.

'Don't talk like that in front of my fucking wife.'

'You stupid fucking cunt,' said Joseph, with a big smile on his face.

'At least I'm not a fucking murderer,' slurred the old man.

'Now please, love, you promised,' hissed his wife.

Joseph seemed to go purple. He tried to laugh. The old man looked him straight in the face. His eyes were raging. I could see it. I could see that the old man was past caring now.

'Not like you lot, you fucking Paddies,' he spat, 'you're nothing but a crowd of fucking savages. You should be up the trees. You're worse than the wogs.'

In one move Joseph was beside him. The bald old man stood still and his wife started to cry. The other man grabbed his arm and tried to pull him into his seat. He was dribbling with rage now. And he was so close to my friend Joseph that their faces were right up together, and their noses were almost touching. They started to push each other in the chest. Marie tried to pull Joseph away. I tried to help her. I swear I did.

Just then, Tony appeared from behind a pillar.

'Now what's up here?' he said. 'Are we not happy bunnies?'

'Calm down, love,' the old man's wife said, 'these people don't want any harm.' She turned to us. 'We don't want trouble. His heart, you see . . .'

'You crowd of murdering scum,' growled the old man.

'What are you talking about?' said Joseph, slapping him in the chest again. 'You know *nothing* about it.'

'I know *nothing*?' screamed the old man. 'Me?'

'Now, now, now,' soothed Tony, pulling at Joseph's arm.

'You're telling me *I* know nothing?' the old man repeated.

Joseph pushed Tony away. He pushed him hard, so that Tony's hand knocked a jug from the table.

'Oh Christ,' said Marie, 'Joseph, please.'

Joseph didn't seem to hear her. He was swaying around on his feet.

'*Nothing*', he said, holding out one hand, counting off on the other. 'What about the Black and Tans? Bloody Sunday? What about the fucking Maguires? What about the Birmingham Six? What about *them*, eh?'

'Let's talk about this in the office, shall we?' said Tony.

'And you,' said Joseph, whipping around, 'you're another cunt.'

'Now look, we don't want any unpleasantness,' warned Tony. 'I mean, tourism's very important to these people.'

'Fuck off, queer,' roared Joseph.

'I'll have you know, sir,' said Tony, 'that kind of talk helps nobody.'

'*I* know nothing,' the old man said, again, turning to his wife. And then something horrible happened. The old man began to cry. His face twisted up. Tears began to stream from his eyes. 'Oh,' he cried, 'oh, oh, oh,' and he wiped away his tears with the hem of his shirt. 'I know nothing,' he sobbed, and he hung his head.

Joseph stared at him, breathing deeply, through his nose. He grinned.

'That's right,' said Joseph, 'you know nothing, you lousy BRIT bastard.'

Tony sighed. He clicked his fingers in the air. Way across the ring, three fatheads in tuxedos saw him. They started to walk over, very quickly.

The old man lifted his head. He turned. He stood for a second just looking at Joseph. Then he lunged. He slapped Joseph just once, very hard in the face. Marie screamed. Tony stood very still. My friend Joseph picked up a beer bottle and shattered it on the edge of the table. He had to hit it twice against the table, because the glass was harder than he thought. Blood trickled from his hand and dripped onto his shorts.

Suddenly the table was surrounded by waiters and men in suits. Glasses and plates flew through the air. Screams. The dancing continued in the middle of the ring. Somebody pulled a knife. More screams. Then the dancing stopped. The table collapsed. I felt a boot connect with my back. I lay on the floor. Ahmed sat on my chest. Marie stood above me, with one foot on either side of my head. As she tried to wrestle off an Arab with a cosh, I lay very still, looking straight up her skirt.

'English hooligan thuggie,' roared the manager, getting Joseph into a headlock and beginning to batter his face very rhythmically against a convenient pillar.

*

The police came to take my friend Joseph away. No amount of arguing would persuade them to let us cart him home on the bus. They'd bring him to the hotel in the morning, they said, just let him sleep it all off. What could we do? He was half unconscious anyway. They promised they'd get a doctor to look him over. The cut over his eye would need stitches.

Marie barely spoke to me while we queued up in the car park. People kept staring. I could see the white soxers, whispering together, pointing at us.

'Come on, Marie,' I said, 'it's not my fault.'

'Well, you weren't much fucking help,' she hissed, 'were you?'

I was a little shocked at her tone, I can tell you. The nerve.

'Now, now, now,' said Tony, 'we don't want any more unpleasantness, we're all on holidays here.'

She looked me in the eye for what seemed like a very long time, even though, in fact, it couldn't have been. Then she smiled suddenly, blinked away a tear, and stroked the side of my face.

'I'm sorry,' she said. 'Friends?'

'Friends,' I nodded, huffily, and she threw her arms around me.

'It's scenes like this,' said Tony, lip trembling, 'make this whole crazy job worthwhile.'

But Tony didn't look well at all. His face looked yellow. He'd have to file a report on the night's 'palaver', as he put it, to his superiors. He made us all get back on the coach, and he said there'd be a singsong to shorten the journey home, and each hotel had to put in at least one competitor. Marie didn't want to. Nobody wanted to, in fact.

'Come on,' warned Tony, 'otherwise it's "Jailhouse Rock" again.'

Eventually somebody started up 'Land of Hope and Glory' and that broke the tension a little. Half-way through the second verse, Tony came over and squeezed in beside us. The bus was cooler now, and the night was dark and black outside, except for the little fireflies which kept crashing into the windows. Stupid bastards.

'A word in your ear, people,' he whispered, 'just while they're all singing.' Tony said he was very, *very* sorry, but there was something he felt he had to tell us. He looked nervous. He lit a cigarette.

'Mr Peterson,' he sighed, 'that elderly gentleman, apparently he had a personal tragedy just recently, so he was feeling a bit upset.'

'Go on,' I sighed, 'tell us.'

Tony started gnawing his lip, nodding. He seemed to be trying to gather his words. He looked at us again, and he smiled.

'Well, it's his grandson, you see. He was in the services, in Germany. Young boy, just in the army a few months. He was on guard duty apparently, one night.'

'Oh no,' said Marie, softly. 'Oh no.'

'Someone was prowling round the barracks,' said Tony, 'I'm not sure of the details.' Tony tapped his cigarette so hard he knocked the tip off it. 'A man with a gun.'

Suddenly I felt very cold.

'Go on,' I said, 'what happened?'

'Well, you see, he was shot, I'm afraid. Twice, in the head. Brain damage – for life.'

'Oh Christ,' said Marie.

'Well, yes,' grinned Tony, 'exactly. I mean, he's a hero. He probably stopped something much worse. But not much consolation to Mr Peterson really, when you think about it.'

'Oh my God,' said Marie.

'They're not sure who it was exactly,' said Tony, 'but, I mean, it had all the hallmarks, you see. So Mr Peterson, well, he's . . .' Marie put her hands to her ears.

'Please,' she said, 'that's enough. I can't bear it.'

Tony's voice trailed off then. Light fell across his face and he looked different. I can't explain it exactly. Maybe it was me. But I saw something in his face that was different. Gentleness perhaps.

'It's my fault,' he kept saying. 'I shouldn't have put you all together. I should have known. Your chap, Joseph, he's just highly strung.' Marie's face was white. 'I mean, I know he didn't mean any harm.' Marie started to cry. Tony held her fingers between his, rubbing them, and she squeezed his hand back, until her knuckles, like her face, went white. 'Come on, chuck,' he sighed, 'chin up, eh? The funny thing is, we get lots of Irish out here, every year, and everyone says they're the nicest and best behaved people. Really. They're known for it. All over the world.'

I think this was meant as consolation, but I couldn't think of anything to say. Tony looked vaguely embarrassed.

'Oh well,' he said, 'it's just religion, I suppose. Gets people a bit worked up really, doesn't it?'

'Yes, Tony,' I said, 'I suppose it does.'

He looked at Marie, with her hands to her face. He shrugged at me. I shrugged back.

'Here, petal,' he said, 'this'll pep you up.' He pulled a flask from his back pocket and made her drink it all. 'There now, girl, that'll put hairs on your chest.'

We laughed, dutifully.

Tony and Marie sang 'We Are The World' later, which made everyone on the coach cry. He put his arm around her waist and they swayed from side to side with their hands clenched together in the air. Tony's voice sounded strong and pure, but Marie couldn't seem to stop crying. She was very drunk now. I could tell. When she came back to the seat I tried to hold her hand again. This time she didn't try to stop me. It was just one of those situations. Tony said there was no need for tears, that we were all friends here, all friends together, on holiday. And everybody on the bus clapped when he said that, which made Marie blush. I put my arms around her, and she fell asleep on my shoulder.

'We've nothing against anybody,' called Tony, 'do we? We're all friends here. Altogether now, campers. We're all friends here.'

Half a mile down the road, Marie opened her eyes, sat up straight and threw up very enthusiastically all over my knees.

*

At four in the morning the muezzin started up, and it sounded like it was right outside my hotel room window, it was so bloody loud. The fan was going round slowly, *click, click, click*. The stench of sewage drifted in from the bay.

'*Allah o akbar, Allah o akbar, Allah o akbar.*'

'What does that mean again?' I said, to Marie.

'God is great,' she slurred. 'I told you before.'

'Oh yes,' I said. 'That's right. I've a terrible memory.'

We listened for a few minutes, saying nothing. Her small hard breasts were white, where her bikini top had kept off the sun. I touched her there and she smiled. Then she put her hands to her forehead.

'I've got such an awful headache,' she said, 'and we really shouldn't be in bed together.'

'*Allah o akbar,*' came the call again. '*Allah, Allah, Allah.*'

'I know,' I said, eventually, 'but we are now.'

There was silence between us then, as she unpeeled the damp sheet from around her thighs.

'Yes, well,' she sighed, 'some things you just can't gloss over.'

I stared at her long limbs as she eased herself out of bed, and walked to the window. She pushed open the shutters and leaned out a little. She flung the condom down into the street. Then she stood there for a few minutes, with her back to me, one hand on her hip, swigging from a bottle of Evian.

'Marie,' I said, 'I think there's maybe something I should explain . . .'

Sweat seeped through my forehead. Outside the window, the sky looked like it was on fire.

'Do *you* think God is great?' she said, without turning.

The pipes gurgled behind the wall. Somewhere I heard the sound of a woman shouting.

'I don't know,' I said, 'I suppose I do.'

'Yes,' she laughed softly. 'It's funny, but I knew you'd say that.'

'*Allah o akbar*,' came the booming voice. '*Allah, Allah, Allah*.'

And we couldn't sleep with the heat, so we made love once more, even though my raw flesh was *singing* with pain and secretly I wished that all of this was over, and already just a part of the past.

Sink

WHEN HE got home from work and saw the washing up undone in the sink, he knew that she had left him.

He sighed a bit, took off his scarf, rummaged around in the cupboard for a tin, sat down at the table, farted. He deliberately avoided looking on top of the fridge, where she always left her little notes. Between the pepper thing and the tomato ketchup thing. That's where she left them, usually, her little bolts of thunder. But he would not look. That would show her. There wasn't one anyway. He couldn't help letting his eye stray. Right in the corner of his left eye, he knew it wasn't there. The bitch, he thought, she didn't even leave a note. He stood up. He let his coat slip to the kitchen floor. He walked around the house, spraying stuff at insects and cursing. He blasted one against the window and watched it wriggle. Then he sprayed some of the stuff on her pot plants, just to show her, all over the glossy leaves. He'd give her greenhouse effect all right.

He opened the letters, glanced at the bottom lines, dropped them on the floor. He made a paper aeroplane with the telephone bill. It lodged itself behind the framed print, 'The Engagement' by Van Eyck, above the gas-fired radiator. For no reason, he cursed. He felt grand. He cursed again. He had never cursed aloud in his own house before, except at her. He cursed a lot, turned on the television, scratched his crotch at the news headlines, bit his lower lip, turned it off. He sprinted up the stairs, two by two, barged into her room. That would show her. Perfume hung in the air. All the drawers lay open and empty. Tights protruded from the wastepaper basket. He lifted the glass beside her bed, still tacky with lipstick. He opened the wardrobe to the rattle of hangers. He knelt down on the carpet and peered under her bed. He opened the bedside locker, but her diary was gone. In fact, everything was gone.

He emptied nearly half the bottle of washing up stuff into the sink and he spun the hot water tap, like a magician. This was his method. He filled the sink with hot water, squirted the stuff, let it drain away, filled it with cold water, so he would not burn his fingers, stacked the plates and all the other junk in the red plastic thing. Soggy cornflakes oozed down the bowls. Bits of fried egg clogged the plughole. He switched on the radio and whistled while he stacked. 'You told me once,' sang the song, 'just how my kisses thrilled you.'

'Since that time,' he whooped, 'oh, how many lips you've known.'

His fingers were wet, so he picked up a teacloth, wrapped it round the cap of the bottle, twisted hard. He poured a large vodka, five cubes of ice scraped from the freezer box, even a slice of lemon. He plopped the slightly blueish lemon into the glass and loosened his tie. He reopened the fridge, leaned in, sent the margarine sailing across the kitchen, clattering into the bin. He put his tie into the freezer box and chuckled. He plucked an olive from a musty-looking jar. That would show her. No more margarine. He closed the door with his foot. He smelt stale sweat from under his shirt. No more rationing the ice cubes, either. He slipped off his shoes and padded up and down the kitchen, gargling the vodka, feeling the tiles beneath his feet, waggling his behind in time to the radio.

On his knees, he tried to think of the word for the smell that came from the cupboard. 'Spicy', it was. Something to do with Christmas cake. Stuff she put in. Secret stuff she said her mother told her about. The old bat. He retrieved a tin of beans, held it up to check the sell-by date, shrugged, placed it on top of the cooker. It was as though somebody was watching him. He wanted to curtsey and to say: now here is one I prepared before the show. Then he slipped her bikini apron over his shirt and cut his hand on the can opener. He cursed again, clenched his hand between his legs, hopped up and down, and sucked the blood from his thumb.

The pot smouldered on the ring, as he scooped the beans out of the can, whistling, throwing the wooden spoon into the air, catching it again, dropping it on the lino. The pot sizzled. He placed five slices of stiff bread under the grill. After another search he found a tin of sardines, right at the back of the cupboard, behind the baking soda and the tupperware boxes of rice, under the mound of plastic grocery bags that she always kept in case they came in handy. He felt efficient. He would show her a thing or two. The key was missing, so he placed the tin box on the draining board and stabbed at it with a carving knife, forking out chunks of fish through the mangled lid. These he spread, with satisfaction, over the smoking toast, flattening the bodies with the teaspoon. Then, using the same spoon, he scooped some instant coffee into a cup, flicked on the kettle, and poured himself another drink. Next he raised the kettle in his right hand, shook it, cursed, unplugged it in again, traced a line down the outside with his finger, held a teaspoon in the steam, looked at his bloated reflection. Then he went to the fridge and got another olive.

He walked up and down the kitchen again, stopped to look at the calendar on the back of the door. It wasn't really a calendar, actually, more of a year planner. He got it at the office. Well, they were always handing them out. There was a little photograph of a cement mixer in the top right hand corner, and all the Sundays were marked in red. He thought she'd be thrilled when he brought it home to her. She could use it, he said, to plan her year. The surface was kind of plastic, so you could write on it, then rub it out later, if you wanted. Or you could use little coloured stickers. His birthday was marked on it. It said: his birthday. That was all. The rest of it was blank, except for Easter and Christmas, which were marked anyway, not that you'd need them to be. She had never got round to getting coloured stickers. That was the trouble with her. She just didn't appreciate anything. If he'd had a little coloured sticker he would have stuck it down, right there, on today's date. And that would have shown her. He picked up the sweeping brush and tried to balance it on the tip of his finger. Then he put it back in the corner.

When he was scraping the beans from the bottom of the pot, his wrist kind of twisted and they slopped out all over the formica worktop. He cursed again. Then he tossed the wooden spoon and the saucepan into the sink. Then, one by one, with a touch of artistry, he arranged the five pieces of toast, each with a mangled sardine in the middle, on two large plates. The plates had pictures of the Taj Mahal on them. They were a present from somebody, but he couldn't remember who. Possibly the old bat. Then, one by one, he held each plate at the edge of the worktop, scraping the beans onto the toast with the edge of an old magazine, *Construction Today*, the special precast concrete supplement.

Licking his fingers he sat down on the couch and flicked on the television. He watched the motor racing, then flicked over to the news, then a documentary about ponies who used to work down the mines, then a chat show on capital punishment, then back to the motor racing. From now on he would watch what he wanted to watch. He forked the beans into his mouth. He did not close his mouth as he chewed. In fact he opened it wide. He wiped his lips with his shirt sleeve. It looked like blood. Then he got fed up watching and turned the damn thing off. He could only eat three slices, and already he felt queasy. He sat back, swallowing his drink, pushing the finished plate away from him with his foot. It slid across the coffee table, balancing precariously, jutting out over the very edge like that truck in the Pepsi

Cola commercial. He reached into his shirt pocket for his cigarettes, took one out, felt for a light, cursed, walked into the kitchen, inhaled the gas as he bent over the cooker, turned off the grill, opened the window to let out the smoke. He looked at the red plastic thing beside the sink. Those dishes would have to be done again.

He walked back up the stairs to her bedroom and he sat on her bed, in the dark, listening to the pipes, flicking ash on the carpet, rubbing it in with his foot. He lifted a long golden hair from her pillow and stared at it. He held his cigarette against it and the smell was vile. He lifted her mattress and looked underneath. He pulled out her wardrobe and looked behind. He groped behind the radiator and wished he had a woman's hands. Then he sat on the bed again, just looking around the room. He closed the drawers in the dresser and sat down again.

Suddenly he got up, walked down the landing, stood outside his own room. The matchstick was still leaning against the foot of his door. He went to pee. He left his glass on top of the toilet, then he came back to his room. Inside everything was as it had been that morning. The strip of sellotape was still stuck across the high part of his wardrobe door. The drawers in the desk were still locked. Of course, she could have replaced everything. Left it just as he had himself. He would put nothing past her. But still, probably not. He opened the window to let out the smell of socks. He flicked his cigarette through the sky. That was a trick he learnt in college.

He unzipped his trousers, let them fall, thumbed down his underpants, threw them across the room. Then he undid his shirt buttons, raised the shirt over his head, and forced his arms out through the still buttoned sleeves. He raised the collar to his nose and sniffed. He sat on the bed and peeled off his socks. Finally his vest, armpits damp, he shoved into a drawer. He scratched his back, stretched his hand behind, then over his shoulder, under his armpit, couldn't quite get it, rubbed his back against the door, squirming with pleasure.

Downstairs again, he sat on the couch, naked, legs apart on the coffee table, sipping another drink, even though there was no ice left, running his fingers across the one single roll of fat on his stomach, staring at his uncut toenails, fingering his navel. He lay back, balancing the glass on his giggling chest. He flicked the television on again, lit another cigarette, picked at the congealing beans on his untouched plate, put one in his navel, flicked it across the room with his teaspoon, giggled. He got a fresh glass and poured another drink. Then he sprinted back upstairs, breathless into his room, put on his dressing gown, came back downstairs. He stubbed out his cigarette on a piece of buttery toast. Then he watched a documentary about people who smuggle bibles into the Soviet Union. The difficult part isn't the smuggling apparently. It's getting them translated into Russian that's the killer.

At eleven o'clock the telephone rang. He jumped to his feet, jolting the coffee table, knocking the plate of leftovers over the edge. He cursed.

Then he counted. He lit another cigarette. He let the phone ring three, four, five, six times. He stood over it, counting. And then he picked it up, and spoke casually, reciting the last four digits of the number. It was somebody looking for the Ding Dong Dial-A-Pizza. They swore it wasn't a joke. They told him there was no need for that kind of talk. They said there was a law against that kind of talk.

He searched the kitchen for a dishcloth, but could not find the one he had used earlier. So he dabbed at the baked beans on the rug with a page torn out of yesterday's paper. He picked up the sardine gingerly, between his index finger and thumb, and scurried to the dustbin. He was cold now. He opened the hot press and felt the tank. All her underwear and things were gone. He slammed the door, opened the fridge, closed it again because there was nothing he felt like eating. The olives were finished.

He ran back upstairs, extracted from the drawer a pair of underpants which had only been worn twice, slipped them on under the dressing gown, came back down.

He tried to read an article on tax evasion but stopped half-way through. He went to the hot press to find a pair of socks. Then he tried to do the crossword, but he couldn't find a pen. He looked on the bookshelf, beside the telephone, everywhere. He cursed. That was typical of her. He just didn't feel like going upstairs again, to his desk. He picked up the telephone book and looked under Rushdie. He knew it wouldn't be there, but still, it wouldn't hurt to look. It wasn't there.

The National Anthem came on at twelve-thirty. He watched. He waited until the very last line, then he reached out the remote control and flicked it off, viciously. He bundled up plates and glasses and cups and walked inside and dropped them into the sink. Then he sat down in the armchair with a very thick book, *The Brothers Karamazov*, by Fyodor Dostoevsky. It was a book he had always wanted to read. He got as far as page seven, but the Russian names were too much. He closed it. Then he suddenly opened it again, at random, to see what word his eye would fall on. He did this a few times, then he put it back on the bookshelf, beside the DIY Guide. Their bookshelf was alphabetical.

By three o'clock she was still not home. He stumbled into the hall, bringing the bottle with him, in the pocket of his dressing gown. He lit his last cigarette. He sat, legs crossed, on the floor. He dialled a number. He watched a tiny spider scuttling across the floor. It rang six times. He said he knew it was late. He appreciated that, for Christ's sake. His shoulders shuddered in the cold. You don't understand, he muttered, I think she's gone for good this time.

Freedom of the Press

WHEN THEY found her body she was sixty, maybe seventy yards down the track, right away from the wreck of the carriage, still clutching a copy of the *Daily Sentinel*. Her face was gone. They identified her by the contents of her handbag, and then they telephoned me from the hospital. Dental records too, apparently. They came into it, later on.

I was still in bed when they telephoned. Two years ago I had to retire early with my angina, and since then I allow myself a lay-on in the mornings. My wife Eileen had a little cleaning job, and I told her there was no need to give it up on my account. She enjoys it – gets her out and about type of thing. That's important for women, even at her time of life. Gives them something to do. Hell hath no fury like a woman with nothing to do.

The telephone woke me. The priest said, Is that you, Mr Guthrie? and I told him yes. Usually I like to hear a new voice on the telephone, because after all, you never know, you might have won something. *James* Guthrie? he said. Yes, I told him, what is it? He went, you don't know me, I'm Father Bob Wallace, the chaplain here at Saint Bernard's Accident. I felt my heart beginning to speed up. He said I'm afraid I have some bad news for you, Mr Guthrie. I thought I was going to be sick, so I swallowed hard and sat down on the seat. What is it? He said I'm afraid it's your wife, Mr Guthrie, she's dead Mr Guthrie, I'm terribly sorry. There's been a train smash.

I told him to go away out of that. Then I took his number and rang him back straight away. Because the funny thing is, you see, I was sure it was some kind of hoax or something.

There's some really kinky people going about these days. Warped in the head and so on. I really was sure. But the phone only rang once and he picked it up himself. It's me, Mr Guthrie he said, Father Bob here. I'm most awfully sorry.

I walked into the kitchen and leaned on the sink. Her coffee cup was still on the table, half full, still just ever so slightly warm when you picked it up in your hand. You could see her lipstick on the rim. I could not believe what I had heard. I just didn't know what to do, so I turned on the radio.

The rail authorities blamed points failure. The unions blamed the rail authorities. The politicians blamed each other. But if there's one thing I blame, it's the *Daily Sentinel*.

The thing is, she *never* reads the *Daily Sentinel*, never. We were married for thirty-four years and it never once came in the door of the house. It's one of those distasteful, muckraking papers, you know, with pictures of young women and so on, orgies, martians, terrible lies about actors and celebrities. It caters for the great unwashed, really, the ignorant types, the lower orders, not for people like us. And still, the funny thing was, when I went to the hospital they said the deceased had been reading a copy of the *Daily Sentinel*. They read out this list, you see, personal belongings and effects. And they gave them all to me in a white plastic bag. Well, that's the kind of thing that sticks in your mind. I got a land, I can tell you. The *Daily Sentinel*, of all things. Why, on that of all mornings, was she reading a copy of the *Daily Sentinel*? What was so different about that morning? I mean, she *never* read the *Daily Sentinel*, for heaven's sake. I mean, I'm all for the freedom of the press, but still, I couldn't figure it out.

They explained the nature of the injuries very candidly and Father Bob said maybe it wasn't a great idea for me to see her like that. Maybe I should wait until the undertakers got to work, tidied her up a little, it was marvellous what they could do. I said, Yes, I don't want to see her like that. He put his hand on my shoulder and said he would be thinking of me during Mass. He was a nice man. He made me feel like death wasn't a way of life for him. I liked the way he put things.

The peculiar thing is, though, on the way home in the taxi I couldn't stop thinking about the *Daily Sentinel*. I didn't know how to feel. I couldn't get it out of my head. It occurred to me that perhaps she read it in secret every morning, or maybe just every now and then, that could be it, or even just once a week, perhaps. Maybe she didn't want to tell me, could have been afraid, or ashamed or something, I don't know, as though I would have said anything. The taxi driver had the radio on in the cab. Terrible about that accident, he said. Yes, I answered, wasn't it? Well, I had things on my mind. What bothered me was not that she was reading the *Daily Sentinel*, no. What bothered me really was that I was so surprised.

I mean, just imagine, knowing someone for all those years. Going through all of that together, all of what we went through, and then not even knowing that they were partial to an odd read of the *Daily Sentinel* from time to time, as though there's any real harm in that. It just shows you. How little we know, I mean.

When I got home I walked around the garden for a while. I noticed that the hydrangeas needed doing again. I noticed that the flowerbed was like a grave. Then I went inside and I picked up the telephone. But I found I was unable to tell anybody, friendswise and family. I telephoned the undertakers and gave them all the details. They were very businesslike about everything, tactful, I mean, polite. 'The remains', was the way they put it. Eileen's remains.

When they had got all the details, I walked into the kitchen. I knelt down on the kitchen floor then and I said a little prayer, just to say my goodbyes, I suppose, to Eileen.

I still could not imagine that she was gone. Then I sat in the front room flicking from channel to channel, to see if there would be any more news. I didn't eat all day. I couldn't. I drank a lot of water but my mouth stayed dry and my face stayed hot. I wondered what I should do without her. The transport minister came on and said it was a terrible tragedy and that the emergency services had been totally fantastic. All very well and good but not fantastic enough, if you ask me. There was going to be an enquiry, he said, to make sure it never happened again. I didn't like his face.

At teatime the telephone rang. It was Johnny. He wanted us to come over and see the baby. He said he'd run us home later. The baby had just said its first word, 'donkey'. I said, Johnny son, I have some terrible news. It's Mum.

*

I walked as far as the station yesterday, wreaths and flowers all over the show, inspectors crawling everywhere, up and down the track, reporters drinking coffee out of flasks and stamping their feet to keep warm. Only doing their jobs, I suppose. The paper man was standing on this side of the bridge and wearing a black armband. He is a dark-skinned man, from foreign parts. Joe, his name is. 'Maltese Joe', Eileen used to call him. She used to say, 'Maltese Joe sends his regards, Jim,' when she came in from her cleaning.

He said, Oh Mr Guthrie, I'm so terribly sorry for your trouble, and he shook me by the hand. I thanked him very much. He said Mrs Guthrie was a real lady, every morning with her copy of the *Telegraph*, every morning, oh for years, so sad. I said actually that's just it, Joe, that's what I wanted to talk to you about.

He scratched his head and told me they must have made a mistake. Mrs Guthrie never read the *Daily Sentinel*, and he should know. He pursed his lips and touched his ear with one finger and shook his head from side to side.

No, no, no, they've got her confused with somebody else, Mr Guthrie, some other lady. She was a *Telegraph* lady, for sure. He assured me that he'd been doing this job for so long that he was certain of the persuasions of all his clients, and Mrs Guthrie was definitely a lady of the *Telegraph* persuasion, no two ways about it.

I went home and vacuumed the front room. Viv said she would do it but I said no, you've been kindness enough as it is and you have junior to see to now. I noticed that the calendar on the mantel hadn't been changed since the day of the accident, and that upset me a little. I found myself looking through our wedding album. The stupid things you do. Then I took my feet off the coffee table because I didn't want her to walk in and catch me. Stupid, I know.

I don't know why, but I got it into my head that maybe she didn't go to our local station that morning, even though Maltese Joe swore she did. He said he'd seen her, but I mean to say, he's old like me and he makes mistakes. It was this *Daily Sentinel* business. Something was different about that morning, I knew it. I rang for a taxi and we drove to the other two stations within reasonable distance. Johnny tried to stop me. He said there was no use only upsetting myself, but I told him I just had to know. Then he offered to drive me, but the taxi was already on its way.

Hartfield Central didn't have a paper shop. And St John's didn't stock the *Daily Sentinel* until late in the day. The stall was hung with front pages screaming about the accident, even three days after. 'TERROR ON THE EIGHT FIFTEEN', said one. 'MY HELL BY LOCO DRIVER', said another. 'WHY' said the third, the *Daily Sentinel*, just one word in big, black, square letters. Why? I bought it and looked at the pictures. That gave me a funny feeling in my stomach.

When I got home I emptied out her handbag into a black plastic sack and I handed the lot to Viv. They had given me her handbag in the hospital, you see, after they had cleaned the blood off. I was going to keep it, but that's just silliness, no point. I gave it to Viv to dispose of. I didn't even look inside it. I couldn't. It was one of our little rules. Mum's handbag was always her private place. I threw the clothes she was wearing into the bin and poured some petrol in there. I set the whole damn thing on fire in the yard. Then Johnny and I went up to the bedroom and took all her dresses and things out of the wardrobe. Some of them I hadn't seen for years. I laid them all out on the bed and started getting them together for the man from the parish. The baby played on the floor, pulling lipsticks and jewellery boxes and little knick-knacks off the dressing table. We laughed at his antics, Johnny and me. Then Viv came in and we all had a big cuddle and we put our arms around each other and said everything would turn out smelling of roses, never fear.

But I still couldn't get it out of my mind. It kept me awake that night. That, and the baby and the way the bed seemed so terribly big. The walls are made of paper in our house. They let everything through. Next day I waited until they'd taken him out for his walk and I phoned up Myrna at the office.

'Oh Jim, Jim, Jim,' she said, 'what can I possibly say?'

'Thank you, Myrna,' I said, 'but there's nothing you can say.'

'I don't know, Jim, death, it's always the people who deserve it least.'

'Well, that is what they say alright.'

'Jim, really, if there's anything I can do. Anything at all to help.'

I said, 'Well, Myrna, there is one thing, actually.'

'What's that?'

I said, 'Myrna, what paper did she read? Do you know?'

I could hear the clatter of typewriters in the background. I could hear somebody shouting for a cup of tea.

'Um . . . I'm sorry, Jim?' I said what newspaper did Eileen read? Every day. She must have brought some newspaper into the office with her. Something. 'Um . . . I don't know. I think now that you mention it, the *Telegraph*, Jim, yes I think so, why? Is it important?'

'Well, it's just I want to know which paper to put the notice in, you know, about the arrangements.'

'Oh, sorry, Jim, stupid of me. Jesus.'

'Anyway, the *Telegraph*?'

'Jesus. I'm so thick. Hold on, Jim.' I heard the sound as she put her hand over the receiver. It struck me that it was like the kind of far-off muffled sound of the sea when you put a shell up to your ear. Funny what you think of. 'Jim? Me again. Yes. The *Telegraph*, apparently.'

'Not the *Sentinel*?'

'What? Eileen read the *Sentinel*? Never.'

'You sure?'

'Just about, yes.'

'Because you know, Myrna, when they found her she had a *Daily Sentinel* in her hand.'

'Oh my God,' she kept saying. 'Oh my God.' Then she asked me how I was bearing up.

*

I stood beside the grave watching them put Eileen into the ground. Over behind the bushes I saw a man with a camera. Johnny told him if he came any closer he'd be waking up with a crowd around him. There were others beside him, with notebooks, smoking, all laughing together. Smoking, if you don't mind, in a graveyard.

When the clod hit the coffin I felt like an empty bottle.

That night there was a knock on the front door. Johnny came into the kitchen and said there was somebody to see me. It was Maltese Joe. I told Johnny to bring him into the front room.

'Joe,' I said, 'nothing the matter, I hope?' His face was white and unshaven, very white for such a dark man, and he held his cap in his hands.

'Mr Guthrie,' he said, 'I feel terrible.' He started to shake. I told him to calm down. I asked if he wanted a drink or something. He said, 'Mr Guthrie, I feel real bad. I have something to tell you.' I beckoned towards the armchair, told him to sit down. He looked very frightened, like a poor little baby.

Then he told me. He said, 'Mr Guthrie, I have to tell you the truth. My conscience is killing me. I had no *Daily Telegraphs* left that morning and Mrs Guthrie's train was pulling in and she was going to miss it. I miscalculated the number of *Telegraphs*, you see, I don't know, it's never happened before, I didn't count right. And when she was half-way across the bridge she came back and she said she just didn't feel like running and she'd take the *Daily Sentinel* instead, just for once. Just for one morning. I told her, Mrs Guthrie, what about your train and she said she'd wait for the next one. She said to me, Joe, I've been running around for my whole damn life, for one morning I'm going to take it easy and I'm going to read the *Daily Sentinel* and I just don't blooming well care. But if she hadn't come back for the *Daily Sentinel* she'd still be alive today, Mr Guthrie, I feel terrible.'

When he had finished speaking he stood up to leave. I grabbed his hand and shook it. Then I pulled him to me and clapped him on the back. And that was the first time in the whole business that I cried. Joe put his hand up and stroked the back of my head. He kept saying how terrible he felt.

'Don't feel terrible, Joe,' I told him, 'you've put my mind at rest.'

Then we all had a cup of tea and a good old chat while the baby toddled around on the floor. We rooted out a bottle of Scotch and we all stayed up late and had a laugh and I felt the weight lift from my shoulders. And the only thing that was missing was Eileen. She would have got a great kick out of it, if she'd been there. She loved a night like that, full of talk and laughter, with the family, she was a very sociable woman. That's what occurred to me later. She was such a decent woman, in every possible way.

I couldn't sleep that night, with the noise of Johnny and Viv coming in through the walls. So I closed my eyes and said a little prayer of thanks to the Lord, because I felt so blessed and honoured just to have ever known her. But they're made out of paper, those walls. That's the truth. They just give everything away.

The Greatest of These is Love

WHEN FATHER Martin Flanagan woke up he felt cold and numbed by a too-heavy sleep. Somewhere in the house he could hear a vacuum cleaner whining, and somewhere else the loud and brutal sound of rock music on a radio. He lay very still. He could smell bacon frying. For a moment he thought he was home in Mayo again. Then he recognised the bareness of the room, and he knew that he was not. His chest rose and fell beneath the sheet. He thought about his dream.

He gaped around his bedroom and yawned, feeling strangely hot now, feeling very uncomfortable. Beside him, the clock on the dresser lay on its side. Father Flanagan saw that it was already past seven, and he cursed very loudly.

'Son of a bitch,' he said, 'what a dream.' He listened to his own words echo around the hollow room. He lay back on his pillow and he stared at the ceiling. He felt the thud of his heart. He held his right hand in front of his face, watching it shiver. 'Son of a bloody bitch,' he said again, silently this time.

Sunlight came through a crack in the curtains. Father Flanagan watched the motes of dust as they danced in the light. Then he looked at the picture on his wall, Joseph the Worker, bent over his bench, sawing at something. He fingered the sleepcrust from the corners of his eyes. He sighed very deeply. He sat up slowly on the edge of his bed.

He padded across the floor in his bare feet, and his toes squirmed in uneasy pleasure on the threadbare carpet. The day looked grey and cold. Cars and long trucks were already moving through the London streets. He watched for a moment, and then he closed the curtains again.

As the sink filled up with warm water, he squirted shaving soap from a can into his hands. It made a farting sound. Then he rubbed the shaving soap all around his chin, his neck, his jaw.

He wet the brush, lathered his face. He didn't really need the brush, but he liked to use it anyway. His hands were still shaking. He was still thinking about the girl in his dream, her thin face, her eyes, her laugh, the curve of her body.

The razor scratched across the grey stubble as he leaned, first this way, then that, craning his head. Pursing his lips, he felt a little ludicrous for a sixty year old man. He looked like he was about to kiss someone. He contorted his chin, flexed his cheeks. He stared for a moment at his own face, the bags under his yellow eyes, the whiteness of his hair. His hands seemed heavy. They felt too large and clumsy.

He tried to console himself. His parishioners believed these hands could change bread and wine into body and blood. Sometimes, even after all this time, he almost believed it himself.

'Father, you've cut yourself,' said Mrs Rocca, offering him a paper tissue. 'I've finished the vacuuming by the way.'

'Just coffee,' he said, 'for breakfast.'

'Are you sick?' she said. 'I *thought* those lamb chops were off last night.'

'No,' he said, 'I'm not sick. Just coffee. Please.'

'And I was going to curry the leftovers,' she said. 'For tonight.'

'Whatever,' he said, 'whatever you think is best, Mrs Rocca.'

He sat in the dining room, listening to the radio news. Things were bad back in Ireland. As per usual. Another bomb, this time outside a schoolyard. And the police over here had picked up some bricklayer in Kilburn. Wanted for a shooting. A judge. Father Flanagan didn't give much for his chances. But he didn't care about that. He had other things on his mind.

Wrapped up in his old black coat Father Martin Flanagan stepped out into the day. His breath turned to steam as the heavy front door slammed behind him. The air was crisp and cold. In the doorway, a robin pecked at the foils on the milk bottles. It looked cruel. Father Flanagan steadied himself. He knew who he was. He was Father Martin Flanagan, the parish priest. Everything, he told himself, would be alright.

In the park, the ducks were quiet as they slid over the water. A breeze blew sheets of newspaper across the lawns. The tree trunks glistened with frost. Father Flanagan coughed and spat. His feet crunched across the gravel paths. He came out onto the High Street, and he turned left towards the church.

In the doorway of the Safeway supermarket a tramp was sleeping. He had a sheet of polystyrene sellotaped over his chest. Up close he looked like a young man, but his face was so dirty that it was hard to make this out. He smelt of vomit. His boots were ripped at the toes. Inside his boots, his feet were wrapped in polythene bags. His feet were bloody. It was London. It was 1989. Margaret Thatcher was Prime Minister, and a poor man was sleeping in a doorway with his feet bleeding into polythene bags. Father Martin Flanagan stared at him, just for a moment. He thought about touching this sleeping man, and offering him something. He looked over his shoulder and saw that there was nobody coming. Cursing himself for his cowardice, Father Flanagan turned and walked on.

He came up the path and in through the back door of the sacristy. The altar boy was already dressed in his grubby soutane. Father Flanagan looked at the clock, then at the boy. The altar boy's skin looked even worse than usual. Trainers protruded from under his cassock. He was wearing an earring. He was chewing something.

'Take that out of your mouth, Johnny,' Father Flanagan said. 'Now.'

'Give me a break, Father,' said the boy, 'I didn't have time for breakfast.'

'Man does not live by bread alone,' said Father Flanagan, 'now get out there and put the music on. We're late.'

On the altar, song roared from the cassette player.

'It's me, it's me, it's me O Lord
Standing in the need of prayer.
It's me, it's me, it's me O Lord
Standing in the need of prayer.'

Father Flanagan walked out onto the altar, carrying his bible and a chalice. The altar boy switched the cassette player off. Silence flooded the cold church. Father Flanagan felt a little like a sergeant-major, telling his men to be at ease. He spoke.

'Good morning, brothers and sisters. I'm very happy to see you here this morning.'

He heard the echo of his own voice all over the huge church. He felt small, but that was fine. There were only seven or eight people in the seats. All old. Most of them women. Each of them sat on a long bench, alone.

'Good morning, Father,' they grumbled.

'The Lord be with you,' he said.

'And also with you,' they answered.

The words of the opening rite came easily. They flowed out of his memory. He didn't even have to read them any more. Still, this morning he found it hard to concentrate. His thoughts seemed to break and float away. It was the dream. His dream was still bothering him. After all this time, still so sharp, still so painful.

'A reading from the first letter of St Paul to the Corinthians,' he said.

He watched the girl scuttle in nervously through the side door. She had long blue hair, a short, black leather jacket, tight leopard-skin jeans. One or two of the old women stared at her, but she didn't stare back. She dipped her fingers in the water font and made the sign of the cross. She looked up at the altar, and she smiled.

Father Flanagan grasped the lectern, and he began to speak again.

'Though I speak with the tongues of men and of angels, and have not love, I am a sounding brass, or a tinkling cymbal. And though I have the gift of prophecy, and understand all mysteries, and all knowledge. And though I have all faith, so that I could move mountains . . .' Father Flanagan paused for effect. He listened to the echo of his voice. He saw that the strange girl was looking at him, with attentive eyes. He continued: '. . . If I have not love, I am nothing. And if I give to the poor, and give up my body to be burned, if I have not love, then I am nothing.'

A dog scampered up the aisle, sniffing at the seats. Father Flanagan heard the sound of embarrassed laughter, and he looked up. When he saw the dog, he smiled. The altar boy looked questioningly at him. Father Flanagan shook his head, and he continued to read, caressing the words as he spoke them.

'Love bears all things, believes all things, hopes all things, endures all things. Love never fails. Where there are prophecies, they will fail. Where there are tongues, they will cease. Where there is knowledge, it will vanish away.' At the back of the church he could see the blur of gold and candle-light. 'When I was a child, I spoke like a child. I understood as a child. I thought as a child. But when I became a man . . .' He paused again. He raised his voice, a little sternly. '. . . I put away childish things.'

He looked down at the girl again. Now her head was bowed, and her fingers were clenched tightly together. Out on the street, Father Flanagan heard a police siren. Hunger rumbled in his stomach. He wanted a cigarette. He went on:

'For now we see through a glass darkly, but then we shall see face to face. Now I know in part, but then I shall know, even as I am known. And now abide these three, faith, hope, and love. But the greatest of these is love. This is the word of the Lord.'

'Thanks be to God,' the congregation replied.

He didn't bother with a sermon. It was too early in the morning.

'Brothers and sisters,' he said, 'I was a little late kicking off today, so I'll spare you my homily and just trot straight into the Offertory Rite.' The pungent smell of the holy wine filled his nostrils, as he repeated the words again. 'This is my body, which will be given up for you.' The altar boy shook the little bells, and their sound filled the church.

Father Flanagan told the people to approach the altar and receive communion. The old women shuffled to the front, and they knelt down at the rail. He placed the hosts on their tongues, or into the palms of their hands, in the new-fangled way.

The young punk girl walked up the aisle. She snapped her head to toss back her long blue hair.

'The body of Christ,' said Father Flanagan.

'Amen,' she replied.

Her eyes were dark. When she bent down low, he could see the black lace strap of her bra, under her loose shirt. She opened her mouth. Her lipstick was purple. He placed the host on her tongue. His fingers were trembling a little. And when she stood up again, and turned around, he could see a line of pale skin above the waistband of her leopard-skin jeans. She looked around and smiled at him.

Father Flanagan felt a strange feeling. Like a fizz in his blood. He dashed through the concluding rite, not feeling well at all.

'Get that earring out, too,' he snapped at the altar boy. 'This is St Stephen's Church, Johnny, not a bloody discotheque.'

•

Father Flanagan pulled up the collar of his coat, so that his priest's collar could not be seen. He went into a newsagent's shop and bought a pack of cigarettes. From the top shelf, pictures of naked women leered down at him from the covers of glossy magazines. On the bottom shelf he saw the tabloid headlines. 'MURDERING BASTARDS'.

On the street, he lit one of the cigarettes, and he stood there inhaling, until the smoke watered his eyes. He watched men and women rushing to work. He watched children hurrying to school. He was Father Martin Flanagan. He was the parish priest of St Stephen's Church. This was just a strange turn. He would be fine again very soon. When the cigarette was finished, he lit another one.

•

'I don't feel well, Mrs Rocca,' he said, casually, 'I think I'll lie down for a while.' He took the cigarette from his mouth and mashed it out in the sink.

'That lamb,' she said, 'I knew it was rotting.'

'It's not the lamb,' he said, 'but I don't want to be disturbed.'

'What if there's a sick call?'

'Well,' he said, 'if there's anything I should know about, just use your discretion.'

'Discretion,' she said, when he had left the kitchen, 'one-fifty an hour and he wants me to use my discretion.'

In his bedroom, Father Flanagan walked up and down. He felt preoccupied. He stared in the mirror again. With one finger he pulled down the skin under his right eyeball. He could see the outline of his skull. He felt mortal. The words of the readings – faith, hope, love – sparkled through his mind.

Outside in the streets of London, the traffic howled. Men were digging the road up with pneumatic drills. They were probably Irish, he thought. They looked Irish, anyway. Then he thought about that girl, so lovely, so young, so strange looking. He thought about the shape of her face, and the white strip of skin above the waistband of her jeans. Father Flanagan knelt down on the carpet beside his bed. He began to pray. He clenched his fingers so tightly together that his knuckles went white. He prayed to the Virgin Mary to take his lustful thoughts away. He asked her to intercede with her son for the forgiveness of his sins. He stayed kneeling by his bed until his knees were aching.

It was useless. He could think the words, but he could *feel* nothing, not even their poetry, not even their emptiness.

Father Flanagan stood up, frustrated and aching. He kicked the leg of his bed. He bit his fingernails. Then, almost as though someone was watching him, he went slowly to his big old dresser. He pulled out all the creaking drawers, one by one. He pretended to himself that he did not know what he was looking for. He tore out shirts and underpants and scattered them across the floor. Sweat formed on his forehead. His heart pumped hard. With one sweep of his arm he sent the pile of books crashing to the ground. Now he cursed, without a thought. He cursed himself, out loud.

He took out the little leather box that was hidden at the bottom of his sock drawer. He wiped off the dust with his sleeve, and then he touched the lid. His teeth gnawed at his upper lip. And he looked at St Joseph on the wall, his head bent over his workbench, sawing something.

Opening the box, he took out the sheaf of papers. His degree, a copy of his mother's will, notes for a pamphlet on the evils of contraception which he had begun and never completed. Under them all, folded into deliberate, creased squares, was her letter. It was so yellowed now that he could not even see the date. The paper was worn away at the creases, so that the first page was almost falling apart.

Almost reluctantly, he held the letter under the light, picking out the tiny, scribbled, old-fashioned handwriting. He paused for a moment, and he began to read.

Then tossing it on his desk in an imitation of nonchalance he stood, crossed the room and stared out at the street again. Why should he do it? He rested his forehead against the cold glass. He clenched his fists and prayed to the Holy Ghost to banish weakness from his mind. Why should be punish himself? All over again. After such a long time.

'Jesus, Mary and Joseph,' he whispered, 'lead me not into temptation.'

But almost as if he could not help it, he found himself coming back to his desk and picking up the letter. Slowly he began to read it again. And as he read, he skimmed over some sentences, and read every single word of others, particularly the hurtful parts, the honest parts, the parts that could still scald him after all this time. The parts where she said there could be no God so vicious as to take him away from her. And when he had finished reading, he began to read again.

Tears began to well up in his tired eyes. They trickled down his face and dripped onto the old notepaper.

Father Martin Flanagan sat down. He rested his head on the table, with his hands stretched out on each side. His fingers clung to the sides of the rickety table, and he wrenched up tears from the pit of his stomach.

'Maria, Maria,' he sighed, 'come home to me.'

Father Flanagan bent his head. In his mind he went back. Things became clear to him. A summer's day. Years ago. Candy floss. Sweat. The taste of lemonade and spit. Music. The darkness of trees. Dappled light. His fingers on the softness of her abdomen. Children playing on the old bandstand. Heat. He closed his eyes and prayed. He clenched his fists. 'Sacred Heart of Jesus,' he sobbed, 'why couldn't she have been more like me?'

Downstairs the telephone started to jangle. He heard the thud of Mrs Rocca's feet as she scurried up the stairs. He heard her shouting his name.

'Father,' she called, 'come quick, there's some poor boy down at the police station who's calling for you.'

'What?' he shouted. 'I'm sick, Mrs Rocca. I told you.'

'But he's in trouble, Father. He's Irish and he's in trouble.' Father Flanagan said nothing. He raised his hands, and he stared at them for a moment. 'Father Flanagan,' she said, 'you have to hurry.'

'Yes, Mrs Rocca,' he answered, drying his tears, 'I'm coming now.'

Father Flanagan stood up and grabbed his coat. On his way out the door, he stopped, just for a moment. He turned and looked back into his room. He closed his eyes. And Father Martin Flanagan could see in that instant what love was, what it was not, and what it could never be again.

He opened his eyes then, and he stared at the letter, its pages spread out over his desk. He swallowed hard at his tears, then he turned and closed the door and walked away.

'Mrs Rocca,' he said, 'that room of mine's in a fearful state. Bloody old papers everywhere. Chuck them all away, will you, while I'm out?'

'Yes, Father,' she said, 'but you better get a move on. They're taking him down to the court soon.'

In the police station he saw the boy. He was young and very afraid. He had short hair and a T-shirt that said 'Thin Lizzy'. He knew nothing about politics, he said. Nothing at all. He just had some friends who liked to get drunk and sing rebel songs and say stupid things. He was shaking with fear. He said he didn't want to end up like the Birmingham Six. Father Martin Flanagan held his hand and said things wouldn't come to that. He refused to leave the cell until a solicitor was called for the boy. The solicitor got him out.

Father Flanagan told the sergeant he'd be watching him like a bloody hawk in future.

'I've got your number, pal,' he said. He had seen Kojak say this on the television once.

Next morning at Mass, Father Martin Flanagan was looking well. Everyone commented on it. Even the young punk girl, with blue hair, who had taken her grandmother along with her. Her grandmother, as it turned out, also had blue hair. Father Flanagan sent the altar boy out five minutes before Mass to gather all the people into the front two seats.

'Take no nonsense, Johnny,' he told him, 'I want the buggers up front for a change, where I can see the whites of their eyes.'

'Brothers and sisters,' he began, in his strong and manly voice, 'I really am *very* happy to see you here this morning. But try not to look so glum. I know it's early. But we are an Easter people, brothers and sisters. We are an Easter people, the victory is ours, and alleluia is our song!'

The girl looked up, straight into his eyes. She smiled. She ran her fingers through her long blue hair. He felt warm. He was Father Martin Flanagan, the parish priest. He was here with his people. He was happy.

True Believers

WHEN I was seven years old – in the winter before my mother went away to England and the life of my family was changed forever – we knew an old woman called Agnes Bernadette Graham. She went to the same church as us, Holy Family Glasthule. That was how we met her, and that was where we continued to meet her for a time, which I suppose was about a year, every Sunday, after that first time.

Glasthule, in Irish, means 'the green apple', so that at an early age the name of this place got mixed up in my head with the story of Adam and Eve, the forbidden fruit, the lush garden of innocence, and how it was a woman who had brought sin into the previously perfect world. When my parents were fighting each other in the kitchen, I used to sit with my little sisters Miriam and Ruth in our big back garden, in the hut that my father had built for us, talking about these things. Because we were children, and because we had nothing better to do, we would imagine together what Eden must have been like.

Ruth said it was probably like Disneyland, full of swimming pools and chocolate streams and castles made of ice. Miriam said it was a place where you got three wishes to start every day. You could use these three wishes to wish for more wishes. And you could use those wishes to wish for even more. You could keep going like this for all eternity, until you had a mountain of wishes, more wishes than you would ever be able to count, never mind use. In Eden, you could have even done this, if that's what you wanted to do.

At that time I used to go to church with my father and Ruth and Miriam, and my little brother, Max. Back then,

Max was still just a toddler. He used to sing in his cot at night, a song that went 'Here comes the fire brigade, dar, dar, dar', over and over again, with no other words apart from these.

I was the eldest child of my parents' marriage, so I was the only one of us who could remember back to a time when they did not fight each other. I could also remember praying to Jesus to send Max to us, because I was so sick of having sisters. I wanted a little brother to talk to, and to teach him how to spell, something I enjoyed doing, and something that was easy enough for me. In later years when Max got into trouble, which he did very often, I used to remind him about this. I used to tell him that if it wasn't for me, he wouldn't have ever got here. Long after I stopped believing in God, I never quite stopped believing that my brother Max was something out of the ordinary, because I had wanted him so very much, in the way that children sometimes do.

The first day we met Agnes was a Sunday, a very cold Sunday in the winter of what must have been 1971. That was the kind of day where your breath turns to steam when you breathe. Or smoke, if you are a child. That is what you think, anyway. You are at the age when you can see the magic in the most ordinary things.

I remember it was so icy that morning that my father and I could not go to play on the little putting green next to the church, something that we almost always did after Mass, while my sisters went to get the papers. My father would show me how to hold the club, how to go down on my hunkers and judge the curve of the ground, how to draw an invisible line from the end of the putter to the exact centre of the hole. But the ground was too hard that morning, so the putting green was closed, the little clubhouse was locked, and the rusty, blue metal flags had been taken out of the holes and put away. When you stamped on the grass, it felt crisp. Underneath that, the earth felt like stone.

So we were just standing in front of the church on that freezing morning, the five of us, my father and Ruth and Miriam and I, and Max in my father's arms, each of us blowing on our thumbs and wondering what we could do. Because although we were too young to be able to admit something like this, we did not want to go home. We did not want that at all. This was because the worst fights in our house were always on a Sunday. And they always ended with my father putting on his jacket and leaving our house, and not coming back until it was late, and we were in bed, and school was just a few short hours away.

My father looked at me that morning, and I could see by the look on his face that he knew what I was thinking. His lips were cracked and pale, and he kept chewing at the skin there, while he stared around himself, at the trees in the churchyard, and up at the sky, as though he was waiting for some strange thing to happen to him.

'Daddy,' said Ruth, 'I'm cold.'

'I know you are, sweetie,' my father said, 'but think of the people in Africa, in the desert. Think how they'd like to be here now.'

'I don't care about the people in Africa,' said Ruth, 'I wish I was there now, instead of here.' My father laughed, softly.

'So do I,' he said, 'if you want to know the truth.'

We stood in front of the church until all the people had gone home, and the newspaper man had packed up his stall, and the young priest had gone through the front gates of the church, clapping his hands together, and into the little house that he had across the road. And I can remember wishing then that I too was a priest, and had a warm house to go to, where there would be no parents, no brother and sisters, no spouse, no one to love and cause you the trouble that this involves.

'Hell with it,' my father said suddenly, 'I feel like an adventure today. Let's just jump in the car and take off somewhere.'

'Do you mean it?' we said.

' 'Course I mean it,' he beamed, 'let's go cause a bit of mischief somewhere.'

'Brillo,' yelled Miriam.

'Gear,' said Ruth.

'Rapid,' I said.

We thought this was fine. Now we would not have to go home until four or five o'clock. Now there would not be as much time for them to fight each other. My father lifted Max high in the air and he laughed.

'Come on, boy,' he said, 'what do you say?'

'Here comes the fire brigade,' said Max, 'dar, dar, dar.'

And I remember feeling the most intense happiness right then. I remember thinking that this would be a good day now, a day when everything might well work out to be alright.

And just as we were walking around the church to get to the car park at the back, I remember being so happy that I began to run. I skidded on the ice, sprinted ahead, right around the corner as hard as I could, with Ruth and Miriam chasing after me, throwing stones, screeching.

'Come back here,' my father shouted, 'please, for God's sake, can't you behave just once.'

And that was when I saw something weird.

At first I thought she was dead. Down beside the gable wall of the church, beside the big black plastic bin where they kept the holy water, I saw this little clump of black clothing which contained an old woman.

She lay flat on her back, with her arms extended on each side of her tiny body. Her eyes were closed. Her legs were thin and crooked. Her skin was white. She lay so still that I can clearly remember thinking to myself, 'This woman is dead, and what should we do now?'

Beside her, on the ground, was an empty 7-Up bottle. It rolled backwards and forwards, and it spun on the smooth ice. My father struggled around the corner with Max in his arms, cursing. For a moment he just looked at the old woman too. Then he spoke.

'Oh my God,' he said, 'that poor woman is after slipping on the ice.'

My father put Max into my arms, and I could barely hold him because he was so fat, and because he began to scream and kick his podgy legs. 'Shut up, Max,' I said, 'shut up, you little fucker.'

Thankfully, my father did not hear this.

My father walked over very carefully to where the old woman was. He put his hands in his pockets. He looked over his shoulder, but nobody was coming to help him. He stared down at her, then he said 'Hello, hello?' in a cautious voice, as though this old woman was a wild animal who might wake up and turn on him at any minute. We crept up behind my father, laughing a little, enjoying the terror of what might be about to happen. For a moment we stood there, giggling, and I could feel my heart beginning to pound. Then I stepped in front of my father and I saw the old woman's bleeding head. It turned, on the ground. It opened its eyes. It looked at us.

Nobody seemed to be able to think of anything to say. So I took another step forward and I said, 'So, what's your name?'

She looked up at me then. She smiled. She said, 'Love, my name is Agnes, and I am the lamb of God.' Then she started to cry. I think she had just taken a fright, all of a sudden. She seemed to be confused and shaken up, and not to know where she was any more. She opened her mouth to cry and her false teeth nearly fell out. She clamped her hand to her lips, and sobbed like a baby. My father held her in his arms. He stroked the back of her head. 'Where am I?' she said. 'What's happening to me now?'

'You're safe now, missus,' my father said, 'you're in the Holy Family church. You're OK. Nothing can happen to you here.' Slowly we helped Agnes to her feet. Her old black coat smelt dirty. She looked around, squinting her eyes, sniffing. She told my father that she had been stretching up to get some holy water from the bin, when she had turned her ankle on the ice. 'You poor thing,' he said, 'you have to be on the look-out for that in this weather.'

My father started to fuss then. He put his hand on Agnes's forehead and he made her count his fingers. He said he wanted to get a doctor, or take Agnes to a hospital. But she shook her head and said she was fine now. She kept looking at my father, holding her hand over her forehead to stop the glare that was coming off the ice, wrinkling her nose as she stared at him. She gazed at his face, as though my father was somebody she recognised, but whose name she could not remember.

'There is one thing you could do for me,' she said then, and she picked up the empty 7-Up bottle. She waved the bottle in front of herself, and she nodded in the direction of the holy water bin.

'Oh,' said my father, 'of course.' He took the bottle, reached into the bin, broke the ice with his fist and filled it up. She smiled when he gave the bottle back to her. And I noticed that for some reason my father was blushing. 'Now,' he said, 'you're set up.' He handed her the bottle and rubbed his hands on his coat.

'Yes, I am,' she said, 'I'm laughing now.'

We gave Agnes a lift home that day, to the little street full of corporation houses where she lived. The street was dirty and there was a burnt-out car down against the wall of the flats, beside a big spraypaint sign that said 'UP THE PROVOS' and another one that said 'PHILIP LYNOTT RULES OK'. Agnes said she'd have liked to invite us in for a cup of something, but the house was all upside down, so, if we didn't mind. No, my father told her, of course we didn't mind in the least. I was disappointed. I would have loved to see inside the house of this strange, smelly old woman.

From then on I used to look forward to seeing Agnes at Mass every Sunday. In the garden Miriam said she was a witch, but I paid no attention to that. I liked Agnes. She was full of strange stories, and just the way she put things was pretty weird. But Miriam didn't like her at all. She said Agnes was a cannibal. She said the reason Agnes wouldn't allow us into her house was that she killed babies in there, and ate them, and made tomato ketchup out of their blood and bones. I knew that this was not true, but I made up my mind to keep an eye on the way she looked at Max in future.

· Little by little we got to know Agnes well. She was always curious about our lives, what we were doing in school, what we wanted to be when we grew up. And sometimes she was curious about our mother too. She asked about her a lot, in those early days, when we met her first.

'She must be very proud of such a lovely family,' she'd say, 'she must thank God.'

My father would go quiet then, and say,

'Well of course, we're both very proud, Rita and me too. They're brats, of course, but they're good kids really.'

He told Agnes that my mother preferred to get Mass in Sallynoggin or Killiney, and we never contradicted him. The truth was that my mother had already stopped going to Mass by then. The way things turned out, she never did meet Agnes. That's a pity. They would have got on well together. I once told my mother about Agnes. I said that my father was very kind to her.

'Oh, is he?' she said. 'Well, he should realise that charity begins at home.'

But later that night my mother came into my room. She sat on my bed for a while, smoking a cigarette, and she said that she hadn't meant what she'd said about my father, and that my father was a good man, and that she did not want for me to turn against him, in case I would grow up unhappy, and never want to get married myself.

My mother was not religious at all. She said religion was all lies and hypocrisy and it brought out the worst of the great bitterness that was in her. She said she wasn't biased, she hated all religions equally. Agnes was different, of course, but one odd thing, she hated priests. She said they were parasites and fools who were polluting the word of God and living it up like dukes. She had that quality of intolerance wrapped up in resignation that you only ever find in very religious people. I used to hear her during the sermon, clicking her tongue, scoffing in the seats behind us where she always sat now. She said things like 'That's a good one coming from him', and 'A lot he'd know about the will of God'.

Agnes had never got married. When we asked her why, she used to tell us that she was still waiting for the right fellow. Then she'd quake with laughter, wiping her eyes, and she'd say, 'Oh God forgive me!' She'd say that a lot.

One day she showed me a picture of the Sacred Heart, with his eyes flaring with passion, and his chest all bleeding.

'See him?' she said to me. 'That's the only boyfriend I'll ever have.' Other times she used to say that all men were the same and she wasn't one bit sorry to be on her own. I think she had quite a thing for my father though. 'If only,' she used to smirk, 'if only you were fifty years older.'

'Oh, now Agnes,' he'd say, 'you're an awful woman, putting temptation in my way. You're a Jezebel, Agnes Graham, and me a happily married man.'

She would laugh then, and so would he. And we would laugh too, in the back seat of the car, even though we didn't actually know what a Jezebel was.

Then one night when we were sitting on the landing, listening to them fight each other downstairs, I heard my father call my mother that.

'You're a hypocrite, and you're weak,' she told him.

'And you're a backstabbing, Jezebel bitch,' he shouted. She cried then. So did he. We could hear them, crying downstairs, in separate rooms now. I knew what it meant then alright.

I promised myself that when I grew up, I would never use that word to anybody. I did not realise that when people are in love with each other, they are capable of anything. This was because I was a child. I was too young to see that.

We never found out what Agnes's age was.

'Thirty-nine,' she'd say, whenever we asked her. She thought this was just hilarious. She'd just fall around the place at that one. But my father told me once that she'd said she could remember the death of Queen Victoria, in 1901. So allowing that she might have been nine or ten then, this would have made her maybe eighty years old in 1971, the eventful year when we met her.

Agnes had this big thing about the devil. She talked about him all the time. She told us one day what she used to do with all the holy water that she brought home from the church. She used it to ward off the devil. She poured it all over everything in her house, to keep the devil away from her. She held up her Coca-Cola bottle, full of holy water, and she shook it hard.

'Oh, this is the real thing alright,' she cackled, 'I always keep a bottle of this in the house, for when his nibs comes calling on me.'

She drenched her clothes and her bedsheets with this magical water. She drank it, cooked her food in it. Whenever she bathed – which Ruth said mustn't have been too often – she filled her bath with it. She doused it all over the furniture and up and down the stairs. She said she could see the devil's eyes at night, coming in through the curtains. Big bright eyes, like Tyrone Power, and a voice, she said, like fingernails on a slate. He was coming to drag her off to hell because she was such a wicked woman. He kept coming to tempt her, offering her all manner of wickedness, if she would only give him her soul. My father had no tolerance for this.

'Now don't be silly, Agnes,' he'd say, 'don't be frightening the children.' But Agnes would insist.

'It's true,' she'd say, 'child, woman or man, it makes no difference to the prince of darkness.'

'There's no such thing as hell,' my father snapped one day, with anger in his eyes.

'Well, that's where you're wrong,' Agnes said, 'there is so a hell, and I have seen it.'

'When,' I said, 'when did you see hell?'

'Jesus showed it to me,' she said, 'a great big lake of fire and ice, and the awful screams of the damned echoing around the sky.'

'I don't believe you,' said my father, 'that's just rubbish.'

'Oh is it?' shouted Agnes. 'Is it now? Well, I'm a true believer, my lad, and on the day of judgement we'll see who's so smart.'

My father told us not to pay any attention to her. He said Agnes was a madwoman who should be locked up somewhere. And the next week at Mass he did not speak to her. I felt sorry for Agnes, standing beside the holy water bin, all alone, peering at us when she thought my father was not looking.

The Sunday after that she came up to us in the car park with four stale cakes, wrapped in a piece of newspaper. She said she had missed us very much and had been praying for us all. My father looked cross. But when he saw the cakes, wrapped up in the newspaper, his face softened and he smiled. He said that we had missed her too.

'You can give me a lift home so,' she said, 'I've grown accustomed to the style.'

Things continued in this manner throughout that year, with nothing of great importance happening between Agnes and us. We would meet her outside the church, talk for a while, sometimes go for an ice cream in the Blue Moon Café, then bring her home to her house. Agnes became a part of our lives. I think we just got used to Agnes, and she got used to us. She gave us religious pictures on our birthdays, and she always remembered to send her regards to our mother. In the back garden, we wondered how much Agnes knew about us, whether the devil really did come to haunt her every night, and if she was some kind of weird magician who could see into the secret part of our lives.

I remember the day of my eighth birthday fell on a Sunday that year. After Mass, Agnes took me to one side and gave me a little parcel, wrapped in blue and silver paper. It was a set of black rosary beads, with 'Welcome to Knock' written on the medal.

'Thank you very much, Agnes,' I said. She smiled at me. Then she touched my face with her fingers.

'You're the eldest,' she said, 'that's a cross, love, I know that, and Jesus knows it too.' The way she looked at me made it impossible to look away. 'Pray to the Holy Family,' she whispered, 'they will see you right.'

'I will, Agnes,' I said, and I wanted to cry.

'You just be a true believer, pet,' she said, 'and everything will turn up smelling of roses, you'll see.'

Agnes kissed me then. She had a moustache. Her hands were like claws. She said I was handsome, like my father, and that when I grew up I would break somebody's heart.

Then I remember another special day, in the summer of 1972, the twenty-seventh of August. We all went out to Bray after Mass, again, my father and me, my sisters and Agnes and Max. We left my mother at home, the way we always did. Agnes was so excited that her face went all red, and we laughed at her until my father said he'd stop the car and slap our legs if we didn't stop.

It was a wonderful day. The sky was clear and the sea was all a weird shade of blue, like the colour of the stuff you put on your knees when you scrape them. Down by the pier the bumper cars and slot machines were rattling, and the sea horses raced in across the waves to the beach. Agnes said the waves were the souls of the angels that God really loved.

She said God let them dance about on the sea for all eternity as a reward for their goodness. Some reward, Miriam said.

We walked up Bray Head. And no matter how much my father fretted, Agnes insisted on going all the way to the top. She wanted to see the big black cross at the summit. We had to stop every twenty yards for Agnes to catch her breath. On the way up the winding path people glared at my father, and they whispered and pointed. I think they thought that he was forcing this poor old woman to climb all the way up this terrible hill. They didn't realise it was her idea. I felt ashamed. I walked in front so that nobody would know Agnes had anything to do with me.

'This was the best day ever,' Agnes sighed, getting out of the car. 'I haven't had a day like this since 1957.'

'Our pleasure, Agnes,' my father smiled, 'we'll do it again some time soon.'

But as we drove up the hill and home that day, my father could not have known that days like this would not happen again, and that everything in his life was about to be changed.

When we got home our house was empty and the phone was off the hook. When I walked into the hall I could hear the tone, growling. I picked up the receiver and held it to my ear. The noise made me think of some animal, but I did not know which one. Ruth came from the kitchen with the note in her hands.

She said, 'Daddy, I think Mammy's gone.'

'Don't be silly,' my father laughed, 'she's just gone out for a message.' He took off his coat and hung it across the back of a chair.

'No,' said Ruth, 'you're wrong.' She gave him the note that she had found by the fridge. She was crying now.

The note said that my mother had taken enough, and that she had to get away for some peace. 'I will always love you all,' it said, 'but I cannot go on with a life like this.'

My father stared at this note for some time, holding it very lightly in his hands, as though it was on fire. He sat down on the stairs, and he read it again. Then he looked at us, and he spoke.

'It's just a joke,' my father whispered. He crumpled up the note and he laughed, and then he threw the paper on the floor, and then he went to the bathroom.

I was not very upset. I knew my father was, but I could not see why. All I could see was that now there would be no more fights. When you are the age that I was then, you do not realise the pain of being left, or the pain of leaving either. You are just too young to know about these things.

When Ruth and Miriam had stopped crying that night, my father went out to get chips and hamburgers. He was gone for a long time. When he came back he had a smell of beer on his breath and the chips were almost cold. He told us that a funny thing had happened. He had run into one of my mother's friends at the chip shop, and she had told him my mother was just gone away for a little holiday.

'So you see?' he smiled. 'I told you there was nothing to worry about.' He put the chips out onto plates and he looked me in the eye. 'You believe that,' he said, 'don't you, son?'

'Yes,' I said, 'I believe it.'

'That's good,' he said, 'that's very good, son. I mean, you know your dad wouldn't lie to you, don't you?'

'Yes,' I said, 'I know you wouldn't do that.' And I was happy then, because I knew I had said what my father wanted me to say.

We soldiered on regardless, as my father put it. At night he would sit by the telephone, waiting, just waiting, for it to ring. When I asked him who he was waiting for, he would look up from his newspaper and smile and say, 'Oh, just Uncle Joe', or 'Grandad' or 'Someone from the office'.

And then my father started coming home early from work so that he would be there when we got off school. He said he didn't want to send us out in the mornings with a keychain

round our necks. For the first few weeks we ate Kentucky
Fried Chicken and takeaway pizza. Then my father began
to learn to cook, out of a book he bought one Saturday. He
burned all our pots and put flour in the meringues. Ruth
said that our mother was never coming back now.

'You shouldn't come home so much,' I told him, 'we can
look after ourselves.'

'Don't you worry about that,' he smiled, 'I like coming
home early. It gives me a chance to catch up on the garden.'
Every day we found him there at four o'clock, raking,
cutting the grass, trimming the edges of the flowerbeds,
until our garden was almost too beautiful to play in any
more. He took us to the garden centre and we bought an
apple tree. The day he planted it, he came into the kitchen,
drenched in sweat, and he drank a pint of milk in three
gulps. Looking at him, I could suddenly see that he didn't
look like our father any more. He wiped his face with his
vest. He leaned his hand on the kitchen table, and he looked
around the room, as though he had never been there before
in his life. He looked like a tired man, who needed to sleep
for a week. 'God, I love doing that garden,' he said, 'we've
really let it go over the last few years.'

One day not long after that, I found a letter in my
father's bedroom, from his boss. It said that the company
understood there were domestic difficulties, but his sales
rate was well down, and if my father's performance did not
improve, they would have to let him go. We sold the car soon
after that, and from then on we walked down to Mass every
Sunday, and I pushed Max in his pram.

'Never fear,' my father said, 'the walking is good for us
anyway.'

One Sunday morning Agnes did not come to Mass. We
looked all over the church for her, but she wasn't there. So
after church we didn't bother getting the newspaper. And
we didn't bother to play putting, because my father had
told me in secret that we couldn't really afford it any more,

not for the moment, not until our fortunes began to change again. Instead we decided to go call on Agnes, just to make sure that she was alright. We walked all together down the back streets to the little cul-de-sac where she lived. It didn't take very much time, because I knew a short cut. My father held the girls' hands and he laughed.

'Your brother has a sense of direction,' he said, 'that's a useful thing to have in life.'

Outside Agnes's house there were four bottles of milk on the step. One of them was cracked. The birds had pecked the foil off the tops. My father rang the doorbell, but nobody came. That didn't matter. Agnes was a little deaf, he said. He pressed the doorbell again, hard, and he rapped on the door with his fingers. Still nobody came.

I stood on tiptoe and stared through Agnes's letterbox. But she had one of those metal boxes on the inside of her door to stop the skinheads throwing shit through the letterbox, so I couldn't see a thing.

My father banged on the window with his wedding ring. The curtains were closed. He turned and smiled at us. Then he banged the glass again, so hard that I thought he would break it, and get into some kind of trouble.

All the boys stood leaning with their backs against the wall, just watching us. They had a radio. It went 'Saturday, Saturday, Saturday night's alright for fighting'. One of them was pretending to play the electric guitar. His eyes were closed and he shook his long hair. The others, his friends, just kept staring. Ruth said she wanted to go home. She said she didn't like being here, didn't like it one bit. I told her to shut up. My father bit his upper lip between his teeth. He started to walk up and down outside Agnes's house, running his fingers through his hair. And all of a sudden my father looked like a child. Or a man who was lost. Or a man in a fairy-tale who had found himself in a strange situation, one that he couldn't understand at all.

'Something's wrong,' he kept saying, 'something is not right here.' He punched the wall, gently, with his fist. He ran his finger around the inside of his collar. He stared down at the milk bottles, lined up outside Agnes's door. He glanced at his watch, then at me, then at his watch again.

My father looked me in the eye. He smiled. Then very suddenly the expression on his face darkened. He grabbed me by the shoulders. He said that I had to go knock on all the doors in the street, find someone who had a telephone, call an ambulance. I had to be responsible now. I had to act like a man. I told him I didn't want to. I didn't want to knock on the doors of these dirty little houses where people were going to laugh at me.

My father took his hands from my shoulders.

'Shame on you,' he said in a hoarse voice, and then he turned to Ruth and Miriam. 'Girls,' he said, 'your dad needs you to help him.'

'Alright,' I said, 'I'll do it.'

'No, no,' he said, 'if your dad can't rely on you, that's just fine, I'll remember that.'

'Please,' I said, 'let me do it. I want to do it.'

'Go on, then,' he said, 'just get out of my sight.'

I did it. I walked all the way down one side of the street and all the way back up the other, and I knocked on every door.

At last I found a woman who didn't have a phone exactly, but she called her husband out from where he was eating his breakfast and told him to run to the pub and get help. I ran down the street after him, trying to keep up. And now there was a crowd of people outside Agnes's house.

The radio was still going. 'Saturday night's alright,' it said, 'Saturday night's alright for fighting.' Ruth was sitting on the kerb, with her coat up over her head. Miriam was trying to look through the front window. Max was crawling in the gutter. As I walked over I saw one man in the crowd take off his hat. I heard a dry mumbling sound, coming from Agnes's hall. It was a sound that I recognised. It was a sound that I had heard many times in my life, and one that I would never hear again. It was the sound of a group of people praying.

I pushed my way in past the smashed planks of the front door. The smell made me want to be sick. From the top of the stairs I saw a big black cat staring down at me. It had bright yellow eyes. It licked its lips and yawned, and it rubbed its back against the banister.

My father was standing in the front room with his back to me. With his right hand he was clutching his left shoulder. With his left hand he was holding a handkerchief over his mouth and nose. A small, frightened-looking man who I did not recognise was standing beside my father, with an axe in his hands. His face was white. His lips were moving, but no sound was coming from his mouth.

The floor was thick with dirty yellow newspapers. The room stank of rot and mould and piss. On the wall, a painting of the Virgin Mary in a blue cloak smiled down, with her hands extended, and beams of light coming from every finger.

In front of my father and the man with the axe, I could see that there was a mattress, stretched out in a corner of the room. As I walked around my father, he put his hand on my shoulder. His hands were shaking. He did not look at me.

Agnes was lying on this mattress, in her old black coat, with some kind of torn-up nightdress underneath. Her eyes were open. Her lips were blue. Her tongue was sticking out of her mouth. It was black. Flies were crawling across her face. Her hands were folded across her breasts, and she was holding an empty bottle. Above the mattress were some words, scribbled onto the flower patterned wallpaper with a crayon. 'Oh most sacred heart of Jesus,' they said, 'I place all my trust in thee.'

My father pulled me to him for a moment. He held me very tight and then he made me turn away.

'Go take care of your sisters and Max,' he whispered, 'this isn't something you want to see.' And when I turned away from him, that was when I saw them. The bottles.

On the floor. On the table. Lined up on the bookshelf and the windowsill. Under the bed. In the sink and the cooker, in every cupboard in the kitchen. All the way up the stairs. My feet kicked against them, sent them tumbling down the steps and into the street. In the bath, and around the toilet. In every filth-encrusted room, hundreds and hundreds and thousands of bottles, some full, some empty, some wriggling with fat maggots and beetles. Coke bottles, sherry bottles, marmalade jars, milk bottles, plastic bottles from Lourdes shaped like the Virgin Mary. An army of bottles, in every corner of Agnes Bernadette Graham's tiny house.

The doctor said it was the damp. Everything in the house was soaked through. It was staggering, he said. It was just no way for anyone to have to live. He pulled the dirty sheet up over Agnes's head, and he sat on the mattress beside her, holding her hand as though she was still alive, waiting for the ambulance to come.

Agnes Graham died of pneumonia, convinced that she was a sinner for whom the gates of hell were yawning. Sometimes when we spoke about her in our garden, I could see the look that would come over her innocent and strange face when she raved about the devil, and the furnaces of hell, and the screams of the damned, and the indelible blackness of her soul. It was a look that I recognised again when I saw her lying cold and dead on that Sunday morning, her body twisted and stiff, with only her legion of bottles to mourn her. It was a look of the most ineffable fear.

Not many people came to her funeral. Just me and my father, and Miriam and Ruth, and a young, pretty woman we did not know, who said that Agnes had once done her a great kindness, but that she did not want to talk about it. It was a beautiful sunny day, but very windy, so that the priest's white vestments kept blowing into his face. My father gave a five-pound note to the gravediggers, because he said that digging graves was hard work, and a task that was not easy for anyone to do. They said they were sorry for his trouble, and he nodded, and shook their hands.

The night of Agnes's funeral I could not sleep. That was, if my memory is reliable, maybe five months after my mother had finally gone away from us.

When I came down the stairs it was late. My father was sitting in the front room, in an armchair, still wearing his black suit. His shoes were off, and his toes were sticking through his socks. My father was crying. His hands were touching his face, and he was softly saying some words to himself, over and over again. And the words he was saying through his tears – 'Rita, oh Rita, oh Rita' – were the words of my mother's name.

This was not the first time I had seen my father cry. But it was the worst time. He sat with his head in his hands, almost as though he was going to suddenly open his fingers and go 'Boo!!' He sat very still, sobbing, breathing very hard, saying my mother's name over and over again, as though her name was a poem, or a prayer. And I knew that this time my father was not playing.

Then I wanted to cry too. Not just because I was upset, but because I wanted to cry with my father. I did not want him to have to cry on his own. I wanted to hold him, and for him to hold me, and I wanted to cry in his arms until all of our tears had cried themselves out and gone away. I could see in that moment that my father was entitled to cry. And I wanted to cry too, but I found that I could not.

That was the night my childhood ended. Because when you feel this feeling for your parents – that they, like you, are entitled to cry – you know that you yourself are not a child any more.

And this was also the night that God died in my life. I found myself in a new world, into which death had come, a world in which death was now a possibility, and a fact which seemed to change the way I saw everything, in an instant of time, the way the most major changes of your life can happen, in a manner that you would think would not be important at all.

Later that night my father and I went to the kitchen and we broke two hamburgers off the block in the freezer, fried them with bread, and sat in the front room watching *Starsky and Hutch* on the TV. He drank a can of beer and I drank milk. He kept wiping his eyes with his tie. Whenever he finished a cigarette, he lit another one on the end.

'I suppose you think your dad is an awful man now,' he said, 'I suppose you think he's nothing but a baby.'

'No,' I said, 'that's not what I think.'

'Yes, well don't you worry anyway,' he kept saying to me, 'you're too young to worry about the big things. We'll just keep the flag flying here, and things will work out for the best.'

'I won't worry,' I said, 'I promise.'

'That's good, son,' he said, and he sighed. 'One lesson you learn,' he said, 'things don't get any easier, no matter what people believe.' He crushed his beer can and put it on the floor, by his seat.

'I'll remember that,' I said, and he laughed out loud, and his face brightened, and he said he was happy to hear it.

We sat in silence for some minutes, listening to the rain that was beginning to fall now, softly against the windows of our house. Somewhere out on the street a burglar alarm was wailing, and all the dogs were barking at the thunder.

My father looked at me, and he tried to smile, although the tears were beginning once more to trickle down his face.

'Did I ever tell you,' my father said, suddenly, 'that sometimes you look just like your mother did, when she was young, and we fell in love together?'

'No,' I said, 'you never did.'

My father bent his forehead, and he pinched the bridge of his nose. He sat like that for a short time, and I watched him, until slowly he raised his head again, and he wiped his nose on the back of his sleeve, and he looked into my eyes in a way I had never seen before. He nodded once or twice.

'No,' he said quietly, 'well, you do.'

And we sat in each other's arms then, until the television ended, and the National Anthem played. We listened to the sound of the rain for a while, hissing into our garden. I suppose we must have wondered about all manner of things, but I do not remember that. All I remember is the sound of the rain, and that I held onto my father very hard, his smell, the strength of his shoulders, the solid and lonely beat of his true-believing heart.